NIGHT
BOAT
TO
TANGIER

Also by Kevin Barry

There Are Little Kingdoms
City of Bohane
Dark Lies the Island
Beatlebone

NIGHT BOAT TO TANGIER

KEVIN BARRY

CANONGATE

First published in Great Britain in 2019
by Canongate Books Ltd, 14 High Street, Edinburgh EH1 1TE

canongate.co.uk

1

British Library Cataloguing-in-Publication Data
A catalogue record for this book is available on
request from the British Library

ISBN 978 1 78211 617 2

Typeset in Goudy by Palimpsest Book Production Limited,
Falkirk, Stirlingshire

Printed and bound in Great Britain by Clays Ltd, Elcograf S.p.A.

For Olivia

'In Spain, the dead are more alive than the dead of any other country in the world.'

Federico García Lorca

Chapter One

THE GIRLS AND
THE DOGS

At the port of Algeciras, in October 2018

Would you say there's any end in sight, Charlie?

I'd say you nearly have an answer to that question already, Maurice.

Two Irishmen sombre in the dank light of the terminal make gestures of long-sufferance and woe – they are born to such gestures, and offer them easily.

It is night in the old Spanish port of Algeciras.

Oh, and this is as awful a place as you could muster – you'd want the eyes sideways in your head.

The ferry terminal has a haunted air, a sinister feeling. It reeks of tired bodies, and dread.

There are scraps of frayed posters – the missing.

There are customs announcements – the narcotraficante.

A blind man roils in night sweat and clicks his teeth to sell lottery tickets like a fat, rattling serpent – he's doing nothing for the place.

The Irishmen look out blithely at the faces that pass by in a blur of the seven distractions – love, grief, pain, sentimentality, avarice, lust, want-of-death.

Above them a café bar reached by escalator hisses with expectancy, clinks of life.

There is a hatch with a sign marked INFORMACIÓN – tell us more – and a small ledge tilts out from it, questioningly.

Maurice Hearne and Charlie Redmond sit on a bench just a few yards west of the hatch. They are in their low fifties. The years are rolling out like tide now. There is old weather on their faces, on the hard lines of their jaws, on their chaotic mouths. But they retain – just about – a rakish air.

Now, in precise tandem, they turn their faces to the hatch marked INFORMACIÓN.

You want to hop back there, Charlie, have another word? See about this next boat that's due in?

Yeah, but the same lad is still on. The lad with the bitter face on him. He's not a talker, Moss.

Try him, Charlie.

Charlie Redmond rises up from the bench in a bundle of sighs. He unfolds his long bones. He approaches the hatch.

He's lame, and he drags the right peg in a soft, brushing motion, with practised ease. He throws his elbows onto the counter. His aura is of brassy menace. He wears a corner-boy's grimace. His Spanish pronunciation is very much from the northside of Cork city.

Hola y buenos noches, he says.

He waits it out for a long beat, looks over his shoulder, calls back to Maurice.

No response, Moss. Bitter face on him still.

Maurice shakes his head sadly.

I fucken hate ignorance, he says.

Charlie tries again.

Hola? Excuse me? Trying to find out about this next boat coming in, this boat from Tangier? Or . . . going out?

A blue silence; a gesture.

Charlie looks back to his friend and mimics the informaciónista's shrug.

All I'm getting here is the shoulders, Maurice.

Habla Inglés is what you say to him, Charlie.

But Charlie throws up his hands and shuffles back to the bench.

Habla my hole, he says. All he's doing is giving me the shoulders, giving me the eyes.

3

Face on him like a bad marriage, Maurice says.

He turns sharply and screeches at the hatch –

Lose the fucken face!

– and now humorously grins.

Maurice Hearne's jaunty, crooked smile will appear with frequency. His left eye is smeared and dead, the other oddly bewitched, as though with an excess of life, for balance. He wears a shabby suit, an open-necked black shirt, white runners and a derby hat perched high on the back of his head. Dudeish, at one time, certainly, but past it now.

You've him told, Maurice. You've manners put on the boy.

Charlie Redmond? The face somehow has an antique look, like a court player's, medieval, a man who'd strum his lute for you. In some meadowsweet lair. Hot, adulterous eyes and again a shabby suit, but dapper shoes in a rusted-orange tone, a pair of suede-finish creepers that whisper of brothels, also a handsome green corduroy neck-tie. Also, stomach trouble, bags like graves beneath the eyes, and soul trouble.

Laid on the floor, between the men's feet, there is a hold-all – it's a fucked-up old Adidas.

All the years we been coming here, Charlie?

I know it.

You think we'd have the lingo got.

Slow learners, Maurice.

Tell me about it. Poor little Maurice Hearne, from Togher, down the back of the class, minding the coats.

Now the bone-tip of Charlie's snout twitches to read a change on the terminal's air.

Policía, he says.

Where at?

You watching? Over.

Fear of God in me. Arrange your face, Charlie.

Tell you what, Moss? I wouldn't fancy your chances in the Algeciras jailhouse. Know what I'm saying? Inside in a mixed cell?

I'm too pretty for a mixed cell, Charlie. I'd be someone's missus inside half an hour. Pedro, come in there, your dinner's ready.

The policía fade into the crowd again.

The crowd is by the moment thickening.

Nobody knows what's coming or going over the Straits tonight – there are disputes on the far side; there is trouble in Tangier, and not for the first time.

There could be hours in this, Maurice.

They won't move until the 23rd. It's not midnight yet.

Yeah, but which end of the 23rd? They move at five past

twelve tonight? Five to twelve tomorrow night? It's still the fucken 23rd. We might have a day to wait it out.

Through the high windows there is an essay on the complicated light at the port of Algeciras. From the glare of the arclights, the lingering of pollutants and the refraction of heat left by the late October sun, the air is thick and smoky, and it makes the night glow a vivid thing, and dense. It is more than heavy enough for the ghosts that it holds suspended here above us.

A tannoy announcement cranks up – a rush of fast Spanish consonants in the fierce Andalusian idiom – and the men are annoyed by the intrusion.

The announcement becomes more breathless and complex as it goes on – we are in the suburbs of hysteria – and, lacking the language, the men are puzzled by it, and irate.

At length, the announcement fades out, and ends, and they turn to look at each other.

That's not telling us a whole lot really, is it, Maurice?

No, Charlie. No, it is not.

Maurice Hearne rises from the bench and stretches out to the full extent of himself. He listens with concern to the creaking of his joints – mother of fuck. He feels out the lizardy nodes of his spine.

How Jesus at Gethsemane wept, he says.

He squints morbidly towards the high windows and now,

with a quick silent look, he questions his old friend; from Charlie Redmond comes a sigh in tired assent.

From the Adidas hold-all the men take out bunches of laser-printed flyers. Each flyer shows the image of a girl about twenty years old. The girl is Dilly Hearne. Her whereabouts now are uncertain.

*

It's about a young girl we're looking for, Maurice says.

This man's daughter we're looking for. The man haven't seen his daughter in three years.

Photo's a bit old now, but she'd still have the same kind of gaatch to her, I'd say.

Maurice? They're not going to know gaatch from their fucken elbows.

Photo's old now, but she'd still have the same kind of . . . Same kind of look to her, I'd say.

She's a small girl. She's a pretty girl. She'd probably still have the dreadlocks.

Dreadlocks, you know? Bob Marley? Jah Rastafari?

She might have a dog or two with her, I'd say.

Dog on a rope kind of thing?

She's a pretty girl. She's twenty-three years of age by now. She'll be dreadlock Rastafari.

7

You know what we're going to need, Charlie?

What's that, Moss?

We're going to need the Spanish for crusty.

Crusty types? Charlie tries. Hairy bastards? New Age-traveller types? That what ye call them?

And, in an aside –

I wouldn't mind, Maurice, but these cunts invented the whole concept of crusty.

On account of they'd have the weather for it, Charlie. Lounging on their black-sand beaches. With all the girls and the dogs.

*

I suppose I do have the odd word, Moss. Thinking on. I mean, lingo-wise.

Hit me up, Charlie.

Supermercado.

What's that when it's at home?

Tesco.

I've a few I remember. Like . . . Gorrión?

Go where?

Gorrión! From a time I spent in Cádiz . . . Did I ever tell you one time, Charlie, I was in love with an older lady, in Cádiz?

I'd nearly have remembered, Maurice.

We used to make love all night, Charles.

You were younger then.

And you know what she'd do for me in the mornings?

I'm all ears.

She'd feed me sparrows, Charlie.

They'd fucken ate anything, wouldn't they? This crowd.

Gorrión! Sparrow!

If it's not nailed down, they'll ate it. Into the frying pan, down the gullet. But it must be class of greasy first thing, Moss? A little sparrow?

Greasy like John Travolta. And not a lot of atein' on them bones, it has to be said.

Personally speaking, Maurice? My arse isn't right since the octopus we ate in Málaga.

Is it saying hello to you, Charlie?

It is, yeah. And of course the octopus wasn't the worst of Málaga.

No, it wasn't.

Not by a long shot, boy.

*

The sound of the night at the Port of Algeciras –

The newsy static of tannoy announcements.

The hard insect drone of police boats on the harbour.

The soft hubbub of the ever-moving crowd in the terminal building.

Outside –

An attack dog barks a yard of stars.

A jet from the army base breaks the sky.

Inside –

A soft-headed kid in singsong makes an Arabic prayer.

An espresso spout gushes laughingly.

And, stretching out his long, spindle legs, crossing them at the ankles, knitting his fingers, clasping his hands behind his head, Charlie Redmond looks high to consider the vaulted reaches of the terminal building, and the vagaries of life that are general.

You know the tragic thing, Maurice?

What's that, Charlie?

I haven't enjoyed a mirror since 1994.

You were gorgeous in your day, Charles.

I was a stunner! And sharp as a blade.

Maurice turns left, turns right, to loosen out the kinks in his neck. Images slice through him. The wood at Ummera, in north Cork, where he spent his first years. And Dilly as a kid, when he'd walk her through London's grey-white winter, Stroud Green Road. And Cynthia, in the place outside Berehaven, on the morning sheets as the sun streamed through.

I suppose I was an unlikely sex symbol, he says. I mean you put this old mug together, on paper, and it don't make any sense. But somehow?

There's a magic. Or was, Moss. There was.

They look into the distance. They send up their sighs. Their talk is a shield against feeling. They pick up the flyers and rise again. They offer them to passers-by – few are accepted. Sympathy is offered in the soft downturn of glances. The missing here make a silent army.

Her name's Dill or Dilly, Charlie says.

She was in Granada maybe? Not long ago.

She might be with a gang of them, I'd say. They kind of move in packs, like?

They move in shoals, the crustaceans.

Dilly Hearne, twenty-three, a pretty girl, with dreadlocks, and dogs, and she have pale green eyes.

Off the mother she took the eyes. The mother was a left-footer from Kinsale.

God rest her.

Green eyes and low-size. Dill or Dilly?

Maurice?

Charlie has clocked a young man's arrival in the terminal. Now Maurice notes it too. The man is in his early twenties, dreadlocked, wearing combat trousers and army-surplus boots, and carrying a rucksack in a state of comic dishabille. He has a dog on a rope. He throws down his rucksack. He is deeply tanned. Dirt also is grained into his skin – the red dirt of the mountains. He takes out a litre carton of vino tinto. He takes a saucer from the rucksack, pours a little wine onto it and offers it to his dog. When he speaks, it is with an English accent, countryish, from the West Country.

Cheers, Lorca, he says. Your good health, mate.

Maurice and Charlie watch on with interest. They exchange a dry look. The dog laps at the wine; the young man pats the dog and laughs. Maurice and Charlie approach the man. They stand silently smiling before him. He looks up at once with a measure of fear, and he takes the rope, as if to hold the dog back. Maurice turns his smile to the dog, and he clenches his tongue between his teeth, and spits a hard

Kssssssstt!

                        *

But Charlie Redmond? He's a natural with dogs. He reaches a long hand for Lorca, takes the paw, shakes it. He bats at the dog with his free, open palm, gently, about the eyes, as though to mesmerise, just little back-and-forth movements of the palm, and the animal is at once besotted.

Maurice and Charlie sit on the bench just west of the hatch marked INFORMACIÓN at the Algeciras ferry terminal on an October night with the ragged young man wedged firmly between them.

All three consider the laughing, the lovestruck dog.

He's a lovely fella, isn't he? Charlie says.

He's a dote, Maurice says.

A dotey old pet, Charlie says. What you say his name was?

His name's Lorca.

And your own name?

I'm Benny.

Good man, Ben.

Benny and Lorca. Lovely. He's named for the little winger lad, is he? Used be at Real Madrid? Around the same time as Zidane?

Little dazzler fella? Maurice says. A jinky winger type?

I always loved a little winger, Charlie says. A slight fella and fast.

Nippy little dazzler, Maurice says. Twist your blood and you trying to mark him.

That was kind of your own style and all, Moss?

Oh, I definitely had a turn of pace, Charles.

You were very quick over the first five yards.

But I lacked a first touch, Charlie.

You were always hard on yourself.

Benny rises and reaches for his dog – he wants to get away from these odd gentlemen.

Boys, I got to think about making a move, he says.

But Charlie reaches out a friendly hand and lets it hover there, for a moment of comic effect, and now it snaps a clamp on the shoulder and presses the young English firmly down to the bench.

There's no rush on you, Ben. You know what I'm saying?

But listen, Benny says.

Maurice flicks to a stand and pushes his face close in to Benny's.

Dilly Hearne is the girl's name, he says. Dill or Dilly?

She'd be twenty-three years of age now, that kind of way? Charlie says.

I don't know no Dill or Dilly! I don't know no . . .

Irish girl?

I known some Irish.

Is that right? Charlie says.

But I don't know a Dill or Dilly. I mean . . .

Where'd you know these Irish? Where at, Ben? Was this in Granada, was it?

I don't know! I mean I've met loads of fucking . . .

Benjamin? Maurice says. We're not saying ye all know each other or anything, like. Sure there could be a half million of ye sweet children in Spain. The way things are going.

Charlie whispers –

Because ye'd have the weather for it.

Maurice whispers –

Ye'd be sleeping out on the beaches.

Like the lords of nature, Charlie says.

Under the starry skies, Maurice says.

Charlie stands, gently awed, and proclaims –

'The heaventree of stars hung with humid nightblue fruit.' Whose line was that, Maurice?

I believe it was the Bard, Charlie. Or it might have been Little Stevie Wonder.

A genius. Little Stevie.

Charlie, with a priest's intelligent smile, limps behind the bench. He wraps a friendly arm around Benny's neck. He leans to whisper in his ear –

The girls and the dogs all in sweet mounds on the beaches and the sky is laid out like heaven above ye.

You're lying there, Ben, Maurice says, and you're looking up at it. You don't know whether you're floating or falling, boy. Do you think he can hear the sea, Charlie?

I have no doubt, Maurice. It's lapping. Softly. At the edges of his dreams.

You know what he don't want in his dreams, Charlie?

What's that, Moss?

Us cunts.

She's a small girl, Benny. She's a pretty girl. And you see what it is? Is we've been told she's headed for Tangier.

Or possibly she's coming back from Tangier.

On the 23rd of the month. Whichever fucken direction? It's all going off on the 23rd.

Is what we've been informed by a young man in Málaga.

On account of the young man found himself in an informational kind of mood.

Maurice moves close in to Benny again and considers him. There is something of the riverbank in his demeanour. Something beaver-like or weasel-ish. He reads the feint blue flecks of the boy's irises. He might not live for long, he

16

thinks. There is a hauntedness there. He is scared, and with reason. Now Maurice softly confides –

You see, it's my daughter that's missing, fella. Can you imagine what that feels like?

Charlie speaks as softly –

Do you have nippers yerself, Ben?

Any sproglets, Ben? No? Any hairy little yokes left after you?

In Bristol or someplace? Charlie says. Any Benjamin juniors left behind you? Hanging out of some poor gormless crusty bird what fell to your loving gaze.

What you shot your beans up, Maurice says.

Benny shakes his head. He looks around to seek help, but his predicament remains his own.

You have empathy, Benny, Maurice says. You're a lovely fella. I can see that in you. So feel it out with me here now, okay? Imagine, after three years, how you'd do anything to be free of this feeling. Because my heart? It's outside of its fucken box and running loose in the world. And we've been told that she's heading for Tangier, Dilly, and she's travelling with her own kind.

I don't know, Charlie says, sitting again, flapping out a lazy hand. Maybe a convoy is going to come together in Algeciras? Spend the winter in Africa, the hot sun on yere bony little pagan arses. Lovely. And all about ye the colourful little birds is a ho-ho-hoverin'. I'm seeing pinkies and greenies and yellowy little fellas. All very good-natured.

17

So is that the plan, Benjamin? Ben? You've gone a bit pale on us, kid.

What I'm going to do is I'm going to ask you again, Benny? Dilly Hearne? Dill or Dilly?

I don't know no fucking Dilly!

Now Charlie folds an embrace around the boy's neck.

You know what I think, Maurice?

What's that, Charlie?

I think this lad is a ferocious wanker.

That's a harsh view, Charles.

Benny makes to get up, but Charlie, with a smile and force, pushes him back down to the bench.

You see what happens, Benny, he says, with all the self-abuse, and this is just my opinion, son, I mean this is just my theory, you know? My kind of . . . morbid speculation. But what happens, with the self-love, it's not just the seed itself that gets spent, it's not just the essence that's lost. What happens, in my theory, and it's something I've thought about quite a lot, actually –

Philosopher, Maurice says. This fella. Charles Redmond of Farranree.

You see what happens, in my opinion, on account of all the wanking, is that the brain starts to get affected and the memory is shot.

The memory? Maurice says.

And clicks his fingers sharply.

Kaput, he says.

And there's no point crying out now, son. Because in the Algeciras ferry terminal?

They've heard much worse.

And I don't mean to be in any way personal with this speculation, Benny. But I'd have to say you have the look of an animalistic fucken self-abuser altogether, you know?

Maurice shouts –

He have one arm longer than the other from it!

And he stands and drags Lorca on his rope, as if to make off with the dog.

Come here, he says. Wouldn't it be a horrible fucken thing for poor Lorca to wake up without a head on him in the port of Algeciras? Like in a nightmare, Ben.

It's an awful place, Charlie says.

It's a shocking place, Maurice says.

Sort of place things could take a wrong steer on you light-ning quick, Ben. You heed?

Dilly. Have you seen Dill, have you?

She's a small girl.

19

She's a pretty girl.

Dill?

Or Dilly?

When the young man answers finally his voice is hollow, weak –

I might have seen her one time in Granada, he says.

*

It is a tremendously Hibernian dilemma – a broken family, lost love, all the melancholy rest of it – and a Hibernian easement for it is suggested: fuck it, we'll go for an old drink.

They move to the café bar. As though on a gentle night's saunter. The young man, Benny, is arranged between them as they rise on the escalator in a careful caravan – he could bolt, but somehow he is reluctant to.

The bar awaits grimly beneath the glare of its strip lights. It runs the thread of its voices. The men sit on three swivelling stools that creak rustily as they turn. This is a place in which time passes almost audibly. Charlie and Maurice sit either side of Ben. They are all three drinking from small glasses of beer. Lorca sits happily beneath on Charlie's grip and tether.

How're you finding Spain, Ben?

It's all right.

Myself and this man been coming here a long while now. What are we talking about, Maurice?

'92, Charlie, I'd say. '93?

Time? It's like fluff on the breeze, Benny.

Benny? Maurice says. You have a grave look on your face.
Relax your bones. All we're doing is having a little cerveza,
wetting our whistles.

Charlie leans down and talks lovingly to the dog.

Who's my number one boy? he says.

The dog lets its eyes roll. Charlie Redmond knows at once
the tune of a dog, and hums it. Now he starts to whisper a
football commentary –

Zidane's on the ball . . . He turn on a sixpence . . . He look
up . . . He knock it in the box . . . Raúl! . . . Raúl misses it,
the keeper has it . . . No! Keeper's spilt it! . . . And it's
Lorca on the rebound! . . . And the Bernabéu is singin' his
name.

Maurice leans in to Benny to address him confidentially –

Charlie Redmond? In my opinion? Is a man that communi-
cates with dogs on a visceral level. You know what I'm
saying by that?

I have no fucking idea, mate.

They nearly stand up and talk to him.

That right?

Now Charlie consults the dog and listens carefully for a
moment.

21

Hear this? He says Raúl was the most selfish little runt that ever pulled on boot leather. Never passed the ball a day in his life.

You nearly want that in a centre-forward, Maurice says. I was the exact same way and I playing inside-left.

You didn't have Raúl's first touch, Maurice, in fairness.

I never said I was at the Bernabéu level, Mr Redmond.

Charlie leans down again, as though listening to the dog some more.

What's he saying to you, Charlie?

He's saying this lad ain't telling us the whole story at all, Moss.

Look, Benny says. Thanks for the beer, but I got to move. Really.

Maurice creaks a fast swivel on his stool and jabs a thumb in Benny's eye. The young man cries out but Maurice moves in to muffle it with a palm across the mouth.

In honesty, Ben? Charlie says. They've seen much worse in the Algeciras terminal.

My personal belief is that it's one of the most evil-minded places of the earth, Ben.

Charlie sniffs at the air, looks worried –

I mean take a waft of the fucken place? You getting an old haunt off it? Smell of bones and ashes.

Are they on their way, Benny, are they?

I don't know who you mean.

Dill? Or Dilly?

When's it she was in Granada, Ben?

Please, Benny says. Please stop.

Okay. We know. All you want is to be at your usual caper. We understand.

Benjamin? Charlie says. He want a black-sand beach. He want to be talking bollocks. He want a circle of swaying dreadlocks all 'round him. He want the girls and the dogs hanging on his every word. He want to be staring all soulful into the moonlight. Ranting his nonsense about the stars and the leylines and Jah Rastafari and the magical significance of the number twenty-three.

The cunt wouldn't go away and get a job for himself, no?

No fear.

Right! Benny says. I'm away.

Maurice leans in, slams him to the stool, bites his shoulder. Charlie muffles the cry with the tips of his fingers placed firmly to Benny's mouth.

Ben? There's no harm done.

Are they on their way, Benny, are they?

23

I don't know anything. I can't help you. I might have seen a Dilly one time in Granada. But it was way back.

Charlie descends in sadness from his stool. He takes the dog by the rope. He moves away from the other two and turns his back on them. He breathes hard as though to control himself.

Maurice lays a fatherly hand on Benny's shoulder.

First off, Ben? I'm sorry I bit your shoulder. There was no call for it. It's shocking behaviour. But I was badly brought up, you know? I didn't have your advantages. I'd say your old man was an accountant or something, was he? Or did he run a leisure centre? Usually the way. With your crowd. With the crustaceans. But me? I came off a terrace street the sun never shone on. I was put out working at four years of age. In Cork city. I was a bus conductor, actually, on the number eight, St Luke's Cross direction. But that's all a long time ago now, and those were the sweet days of my youth and they're not coming back. Oh, no, they are not. And never did I think I'd wind up the way I am now. A man that's heartbroken. A man that hasn't seen his Dilly in three fucken years. Imagine what that does to a fella? But I apologise again, Benny. I do. Are we on speaking terms?

Benny half nods; he's very scared.

Well, listen to me carefully and take good heed, okay? Because you see that man there? Charlie Redmond? Of Farranree? See what he's trying to do there? He's trying to control his breaths, Ben. He's trying to articulate his spine.

24

He calls over to Charlie –

Are you articulatin' your spine, Charles?

If there's nothing else I'm doing, I'm articulatin' my cunten spine, Moss.

That's good news, Ben, because if he don't relax himself? All bets are off. I mean seriously. Charlie Redmond? A gentleman. A philosopher. A man so attuned to emotions he can communicate on a bodily level with the most delicate creatures of us all, which is dogs. Charlie Redmond? Loyal as an old dog himself, and fierce! If needs be. And I tell you now, since she were no bigger than a little trout? Dilly Hearne has been that man's darling. Oh, he doted on her. He was around our place four nights of the week, five, bringing her comic books, DVDs, sneaking her in sweets, and if he didn't show up, of an evening, she'd be at the window, upstairs, looking out, where's my Unkie Charlie? And it's three years now since we seen Dilly, and you can imagine what it's like for me, the girl's father, I've been in hell. But Charlie Redmond? He's as bad again. No peace, no solace, not till his Dilly's got back to him.

Charlie returns to the pair, with the happy dog, and he squats in front of Benny. He opens his suit jacket, takes out a knife, looks around carefully. He shows the knife to Benny, both sides of it. He puts it inside his jacket again.

I'd hate to have to take the head off the fucken dog, Ben, you know what I'm saying? So tell me now. Is Dilly due in, is she? Dilly Hearne?

She's a small girl.

She's a pretty girl.

*

On the bench just west of the hatch marked INFORMACIÓN, Maurice and Charlie again sit at either side of Benny. Charlie has the dog on the rope and sings to it quietly.

From when she was about thirteen or fourteen? Maurice says. It was all going a bit amateur dramatics with Dilly. Scarification. Voices in the night. Running away to the Ummera Wood and burying herself alive. Not calling her mother nor me. Not so much as a text message. We're going up the walls. Her ladyship is buried to the shoulders in the fucken dirt. And that was hard, Ben, it was, to be dealing with the Oscar-winnin' performances, because when she was younger? She was just . . .

A dote, Charlie says, to break his song.

A gorgeous little one. Watch a bit of telly with you. Laughing her head off. The little chuckles? I can hear them in my chest still.

Is she on her way, Ben?

But the next thing, Maurice says, she's fourteen years of age and she's after getting into the music and books on white magic and the bedroom door is locked and she's sat in there like a fucken compost heap. Face on her.

The way it's happening, Charlie says, is there's a convoy of ye getting together in Algeciras. Some are heading out for

Tangier and others are coming back. It's got to do with who minds the dogs. At least this is what our friend in Málaga has us believe.

You hitting over to Morocco for the winter, Ben?

Someone come back and mind the dog for you? That how it works? And ye move on the 23rd of the month always.

On account of the magical significance of the number, Maurice says.

You think we're going to let Morocco happen, Ben?

You think we don't know what Morocco's like? A girl gets lost in that place and she could stay lost forever.

We been in and out of Morocco since 1994, son.

Charlie Redmond? This man here? The only man I ever heard of that smuggled dope *into* Morocco.

Oh, lots of old stories, Ben, lots of adventures. This fella? Maurice Hearne? Do you know you're looking at a fella there who's worked in the High Atlas trading goats for dope?

The stories we could tell, Benny. Did you ever try and buy 350 goats off a fella from Marrakesh, did you?

On credit.

In a Cork accent.

Morocco? We know the ins and outs of that place years since.

Now Maurice rises and stands directly in front of Benny.

Where are all the girls and the dogs, Benny?

For why have they forsaken you, Benjamin?

Look! Once or twice. Ever! That's all I ever talked to Dilly. And it was a while back.

Pale green eyes she got, Maurice says. Off Cynthia she took the eyes, who was a left-footer, from Kinsale, because I married up, Ben. You'd think she'd have passed on a few decent Protestant manners to the girl?

She don't say much, Benny says. From what I saw of her. She kept to herself mostly.

A breakthrough – Maurice and Charlie smile at the boy; they are fond now, avuncular.

She made the disks of the sun, Benny says.

She made the fucken what?

They call them sun disks. What the girls make. They're like wooden . . . pendants? For around the neck. The girls burn the designs on with a magnifier, on hot days. Then it's one for ten euros, three for twenty. At the markets and that.

Jesus Christ, Maurice says.

Easy, Moss.

You know that girl got nine honours in her Junior Cert, Charlie?

Leave it go, Maurice.

It's hard to, Charles! A girl of infinite fucken possibility!
And you turn around and she's out the gap and gone to
fucken Spain and hanging off hairy bastards and selling tat
at the side of the road like a fucken leper! And I mean at
twenty-three years of age? She's a pure fucken gom still!
She's a gommie lackeen! A fucken sweeping brush handle
with a mickey attached to it could talk her into Morocco!

Why'd she take off? Benny says. You ask yourself that ever?

Maurice and Charlie exchange a brace of silken grins.

Ho ho, Maurice says.

Charlie limps soulfully around back of the bench and rests a
palm on Benny's shoulder. He speaks calmly and kindly.

I don't know if you're getting the sense of this yet, Ben. But
you're dealing with truly dreadful fucken men here.

Maurice leans in, smiling broadly.

We're an awful pair, he says.

Deranged, Charlie says. Devil-sent.

What time were ye thinking of crossing over, Ben? What
boat are ye on? Is that decided?

Is the girl Dilly due in Algeciras, Ben?

Now the echo of a dog's bark opens a hollow nearby.
Benny looks hopefully towards it. Maurice and Charlie look
at each other; Charlie holds Lorca back on the rope.

Two girls appear.

Their hair is worn in dreadlocks and they carry heavy rucksacks.

Their clothes are ragged, their skins nut-brown.

One of the girls has a dog on a rope.

Chapter Two

THE TATTOOED TIT

In the city of Málaga, and beyond, in January 1994

At the Café Central, in the Plaza de la Constitución, he drank café solo and waited. Around him there was the ceaseless hum of the old Andalusians' talk. They balled up their napkins and threw them to the tiled floor. The old men spat, narrowing their faces. Their skins of almond shade. The air was blue with cigarette smoke that rose in slow drifts. The old ladies wore ankle-length fur coats for the winter sun. They had high comical arched eyebrows painted on and looked perpetually startled. The coffee machines laughed and spat also. The patrons drank café solo and con leche and cortado and hot chocolate, and ate sugary lengths of long, twisted churros. A woeful fat man from Birmingham arrived just a few minutes late. He had a look of high moral injury as he took a seat opposite Maurice Hearne. His great, fleshy frame came to rest in a soft stack of complaint.

You're a bloody daft child, he said. If you had any sense, you'd get up right now and run a fast mile. And you would not look back, Maurice. You would not look fucking back.

He ordered chocolate and a ración of the churros and fed on them with tiny anxious bites. He spoke lowly, as if they might be spied on. He borrowed a pen from the waiter and tore a scrap of paper from the waiter's pad and passed these to Maurice. He recited slowly the details and number of a bank account, and it was in a half-sung drone, as if he were praying. There were no two ways of doing it, he said. It was half the money first and then he would be allowed to meet Karima.

You want your bloody daft Irish head examined, he said. And I mean no offence, son, because my mother was from County Mayo. But these people? These people are a sensationally bad idea. I know of what I speak. You're swimming out of your water. You should throw away that piece of paper. You should forget you've ever seen my plain little face. Because these people, Maurice? Oh, sweet Jesus God, no.

He paid for Maurice's coffee and shook his hand tightly as he stood to leave.

Rethink it, he said. Go home. Have your life. Get a job of gainful. Make some bloody kiddies.

Alone again, Maurice watched himself in the café as though from a distance. His vision was blurred at the edges – the fear. The crowd thinned out. The Spanish cafés ran on unlearnable hours. Here we're all in; here we're all out again. Fur coats trailed on the tiled floor. Sombre waiters in white shirts swept up the napkins and the cigarette butts. The head waiter looked like a 'tacheless Salvador Dalí and drank a ball of coñac and was sustained. It was like a funeral; the sad Andaluz faces. Maurice drained the last cold beads of his coffee and left.

It was dusk already in the street and he walked in the full gloom of youth and the sparrows bickered among themselves clannishly and hopped gaily from the bins. On the Alameda Principal he walked under palm trees still strung with Christmas lights to spell FELICIDADES, and he was aroused by the fear and by the scale of the money, both. He liked the happy mysterious babble of the evening streets, and he tried to distinguish some words. Vah-lay, he heard again and again – vah-lay – and it sounded regretful, a sigh. In a bar on the Alameda he fed coins to a phone on the counter and called the hallway phone in the old house of flats at St Luke's Cross. He felt her hurry down the stairs to answer, down that haunted stairwell, and he counted off the steps, eight, nine, ten, to the softness of her voice –

Did you see him?

Oh, I fucken did, yeah. Jesus Christ.

Really?

A big sweating Brummie fuck. Kept telling me to go the fuck home out of it.

So is this it, do you think?

It'll be tomorrow. I think it'll be fine.

It isn't too late not to.

Cynthia, it'll be fine. It's farming.

Ah but Maurice listen to me.

I miss you. I badly want to see you.

Yeah well that's all fantastic until.

It's going to be okay. I'll be back soon. I can hear you still.

The city ran a swarm of fast anchovy faces. The surge of the night traffic ran. The harbour lights were festive and moved across the oily water. He walked as far as the beach of Malagueta to get his head right and let the fear settle. He recognised at once that there was heroin in the vicinity of Malagueta by night. The heavy sea was constrained on tight lines. He sat in the dark on the sand and listened to the night, the traffic; the fast, sibilant hiss of the Andaluz voices.

He reasoned that if he didn't sleep, there was no way he could dream about his father.

*

Karima was about forty and thin and kind of good-looking in a skanky way and with sexy bad teeth when she opened her mouth to take in huge, derisive gulps of her cigarette smoke, as if it couldn't possibly feed the burning want of her Saharan lungs. Her thin face folded to a grimace on the intake, creased again to smile as she exhaled. She steered her small, neat car through the new suburb set high in the Málaga hills.

You have a face, she said. It's like what you call in the films? In the fairy story? In the Walt Disney?

I don't know if I like the sound of this, Maurice said.

I mean the little creature, she said. In the woods. The word?

She shook her head as she drove – she could not find the word. She turned onto an unfinished road at the top of the new development. Large, ominous birds hovered to hunt above the red dirt of the hills. There was a sensation of lizards. The white apartments were clean as picked bone and appeared to be untenanted – there were no cars. Way beneath them the Mediterranean was brilliant in the winter sun.

Elf! she said.

Okay, he said.

You are an elf, she said. Your face.

I take no offence, he said. You mean that I have an elfin look. Is what you're trying to say to me.

Elfin?

Meaning elf-like, he said, or with elf-type characteristics.

And certainly they were by this point wondering what it would be like to fuck each other.

Very strange, she said.

His mother always said they must have found him in the Ummera Wood. Even as a kid, in the stroller, he was tuned to odd frequencies, it seemed. Karima parked the car beside a raw apartment unit as yet unplastered. There were no people anywhere to be seen. She wore low-rider jeans and a pale lemon Adidas polo; he did not recognise the make of the trainers. She lit another cigarette and smiled at him to show her awful, yellow, alluring teeth, also the warm dark of her maw. She brought him inside the unfinished apartment and there displayed a hundred kilos of graded Moroccan hashish stacked neatly. The extent of it certainly was agricultural. She said that tonight or even the next few days would be good. He could send his people. They could get together at the port of Málaga late on.

And this is the way it will go, she said. You don't ever need to see Tangier.

They went outside again and got into her car. She went by a different route and turned down an unpaved avenue.

Something else we see, she said.

She brought him to another unfinished apartment. As soon as she unlocked the door, he could smell the stench of human filth. A man wearing just a pair of yellow vinyl football shorts was chained to the chrome leg of a kitchen island – he was blindfolded also and gagged. There was no furniture; the walls were unplastered. The man moaned dully and rolled over to show his bound mouth. He was slick with pain. There was a long, dark bruise running half the length of his thigh.

Okay, she said, and they left again.

They got back in the car and she smiled.

This is also how it goes sometimes, she said.

Ah, yeah, Maurice said.

She shook her head slowly – her regret was sweet, girlish.

He's French, she said. They're all cunts.

You'd hear that all right, Maurice said.

*

She drove him to a bar in the mountains. It was deserted
but for the owner. He was a reedy, grave man in late middle
age. He looked as if it were all turning out just as he'd been
warned. A Catholic, in other words, and he was absorbed by
a mystic lady who spoke in a deep, husky tone on a small
TV playing above the counter. Maurice lacked the language,
but he could sense easily that the mystic was conversing
with the dead. She hovered her palms above snapshots of
elderly Spaniards. Souls as nothing but the husks of
Polaroids. Even as he filled their glasses from the beer tap,
the sombre owner did not take his eyes from the screen.

Do you believe in the dead? Karima said.

How'd you mean?

You think they can see us?

Down here?

Yes.

Right now?

Yes.

I fucken hope not.

Maybe they can just hear us, she said.

Karima came from the Rif Mountains, but she lived now in Málaga. When she turned to look up at the TV again, he arranged a glimpse down the front of her polo shirt. At the top of the left tit was inked a tiny '13'. He knew that she would be a great presence in his life. By a sort of sensual divination he knew this. A phone number streamed across the bottom of the screen beneath the mystic lady, and the barman took a pen from behind the register to make a note of it.

Karima turned to Maurice, and she smiled as she found him down her shirt front.

Why would you think of that now? she said.

On the screen the mystic put her hands to her face and exclaimed desperately – she made a sudden, piercing sound, eerie as an owl's hoot. Messages from elsewhere, apparently.

There is nothing fucking good coming through, Karima said.

Well, this is it, Maurice said.

*

Charlie Redmond flew in the next day. Charlie Red had never been on a plane before. It seemed to have raised him a notch higher in self-confidence levels – a notch that he did not need. First night, he was up and down the Alameda Principal acting like he was number one. His snout in the air, the shoulders moving, turning to check out the Spanish girls going by, nodding slowly and serenely as they went by, like a connoisseur taking the waft of something precious and rare. He wore a two-piece velour Gio-Goi tracksuit, a Kangol slouch hat and some kind of Brazilian – fucken *Brazilian* – trainers. The soles were made out of virgin rubber, Charlie had confided, with soft wonder in his voice. Charlie every month bought The Face and i-D magazines, spent hours on the fashion layouts, poring over them, with an expert's keen and rueful air.

Are you trying to look like you're involved in the fucken drug business? Maurice said.

Drug business? Charlie said. I'm import–export. I've flown in for a trade show.

They were in a bar on the Alameda, drinking beer and eating tapas.

What's this bollocks, Moss?

Octopus, Charlie.

You windin' me up?

Can you not see it? Look? It's got all the little tentacles and shit?

And we're supposed to be atein' that? This crowd would want to cop themselves on altogether.

Nervously he took a bite, chewed suspiciously for a moment, then relaxed into it with a warm, open smile.

Gorgeous, he said.

But beneath Charlie's left eye there was a tic of nervous

fluttering, as if a tiny bird were trapped beneath the skin, and it signified that the night was a heavy one.

They took a taxi down the port to see Karima's people and to arrange the transportation.

We play it like it's the nine hundred and eighty-ninth time we've done this, Maurice said, and not the first.

Charlie Redmond did not need telling. The thing about Charlie was that you took him into a room and they knew. One look and they fucking knew. A single glance into the soulful eyes of Mr Charles Redmond, and they knew that this could go in any direction.

At the port of Málaga the night sky was bled out pale, and the anchor lines and the rigging of the off-season yachts made a nervous chatter in the breeze. In the throw of the arclights the gulls hovered with comic, gruesome eyes. After a short wait a jeep pulled up, and a heavy-set, smiling driver beckoned them with a broad, pantomime gesture.

We're on, Maurice said.

Chapter Three

COAST OF BARBARY

At the port of Algeciras, in October 2018

The girls with the dog turn out to be witches from the province of Extremadura.

Which is a turn-up for the books, says Charlie Redmond.

The girls' names are Leonor and Ana. Their English is limited. Their dog is named Junior Cortés. Their smiles are glazed and alive. Their ink shows symbols of the occult. They claim not to know Benny from previously; Benny agrees that he has never seen these particular girls before. Lorca and Junior Cortés are wary of each other but also interested. It's as if a little family is coming together.

Maybe that's all that's wrong with us in the first place, Charlie says. Families. Or the absence of.

Maurice returns suavely from the concession with three bottles of cheap cava and paper cups.

Either we elevate ourselves from the beasts of the fields, he says, or we eat our fucken guns.

Dilly Hearne is the girl's name, Charlie says. Dill or Dilly?

Three years she's been gone, Maurice says, and here's me, her old dad, with the heart hangin' sideways out of me chest.

We're going to need the Spanish for crusty, Moss. She took off with yere own kind, girls . . . Ye know what I'm saying?

She was in Granada maybe? Not long ago?

I don't know Dilly, Leonor says.

We just come from Cádiz, Ana says.

Cádiz! Maurice says. Did I ever tell ye one time I was in love with an older lady in Cádiz?

There wasn't a sparrow safe for miles, Charlie says.

Gorrión! Maurice cries, and pours the drinks with an excess of wristy flourishes.

Leonor and Ana laugh uneasily and accept the drinks and sip at them. Benny takes a drink and finds that it steadies the nerves. The dogs relax into each other and lie back. The night ages. The port of Algeciras has seen stranger times. Now Maurice and Charlie find themselves on the precipice of a great reminiscence. (Algeciras, always, is a reminiscent town.)

Families? Maurice says. Don't be talking to me about families.

Maurice Hearne? Charlie says. A man that's been through the ringer like ye wouldn't fucken believe.

Maurice stands, shows in a sad smile his earned wisdom, and gazes towards the high windows.

Did ye know there are only seven true distractions in life? he says.

Name 'em, Moss.

Top banana? The want-of-death.

Of course it is, Charlie says.

We know this, Maurice says. We're all looking for the ticket to ride. And there's lust, certainly, because we all want to get our ends away.

At some sort of reasonable level anyhow, Charlie says.

I fully accept there's a thing called love, Maurice says. Haven't I been half my born days up to my sucker eyeballs in it? And there's sentimentality, which is all tied up with the love and the lust. There's grief and the longer we go on, the more of it we've the burden of.

It accretes, Charlie says, like a motherfucker out of control. Does the old grief.

There's pain, Maurice says. Mental and physical divisions.

My stomach is talking to me, Charlie says, and my arse is only trotting after it.

I had the dry heaves there a while ago, Maurice says, and a mystery pain out my left lung.

Will we go into the mental, Moss?

No, we will not, Mr Redmond. Because we'd be here for the fucken night.

You've only listed six, Maurice. Of the distractions.

On account of I'm leaving the kicker till last, Charlie.

Being?

Being avarice, Charles. Being our old friend avarice.

*

The night is slowly passing. There is no word on the next boat. There are difficulties at port on the Tangier side. Difficulties are not unknown on either side. There is no sign of Dilly Hearne. Charlie Redmond knits his long, bony fingers behind his head. He is patient as a statue. Maurice Hearne turns his derby hat in his hands and considers its slowly turning rim, as if all the years are turning back.

This old Charlie? he says. A man with a very attractive personality. In lots of ways. I'm not saying he's an angel. I mean back in the day? We were an awful pair. Savages. Oh, what we didn't get up to? And there was a lot of money, which complicates everything. That's when our old friend avarice comes a knock-knock-knockin' along.

Shoot-the-bastard, shoot-the-bastard, Charlie says.

Ah, listen, my sweet darlings. The stories I could tell ye? About what I've been through? You wouldn't put an idle fucking dog through it. No offence, Lorca. No offence, Junior Cortés. You see the money comes into everything. You have to do the accounts at some stage. You have to settle the books. And, actually, me and this fella, we go back so long, we were in the same classroom together. We did Inter Cert-level business studies together. Biz org! Isn't that what we used call it, Charlie? Tuesday morning, double biz org, you'd have the eyes clawed out of your head. This is in Cork city I'm talking about, the rain outside, oh, it's heaving down. Ferocious little self-abusers. The haircuts on us! And we trying to crawl up the Prez Convent skirts. Till the eyes were crooked in our heads. The waft of it alone enough to break a boy's heart.

Estuarine, Charlie Redmond says.

But over the years? What happened was the money. There was a lot of money. Oh, it was really moving for us. Whatever way our luck turned? The horse was after coming in at forty-to-one. Metaphorical speaking. There was a lot of money, and I'm not saying for one minute that Cynthia shouldn't have had a lovely house to her name and our daughter well looked after. And of course we needed to have the money coming in the way it was coming. Charlie had his exes that were being catered for.

The likes of Fiona fucken Condon? Charlie says. The woman like a pump the way she suck money out of you. And I paying out for her children from a previous? Three thousand, eight hundred euro a month at one stage I had going out to Fiona Condon alone. The young fella need football boots, et cetera. Do he need 'em made out of fucken gold? Unbelievable.

There was a lot of money unaccounted for, Maurice says. It remains so. Cynthia couldn't have spent it all. Despite her very best efforts. And I'm not saying for one minute she didn't deserve her comforts. The fucken sofas she had going on? She was going to Copenhagen for the sofas. And, in my opinion, the woman deserved it all, and more.

Dilly Hearne, Charlie says. She's a small girl. She's a pretty girl.

She may just possibly have done us over, Maurice says.

It's in her blood to, Charlie says.

Green eyes, Maurice says. Off the mother she took a lovely set of Protestant eyes.

Cynthia. God rest her. She'd the palest green eyes.

They were like the fucking sea, Maurice says.

*

Their talk comes in slow drifts, then in quicker attacks. It builds up; it spins out. Leonor and Ana know by experience the patience required for the port of Algeciras when the boats are uncertain, and they know too the strangeness that gathers here always – soon they lie sleeping against their packs. The dogs also are sleeping. Benny is more wary than the girls and cannot sleep – he watches for a gap to open. Maurice lies back across the bench, as though laid out for the deadhouse, with his hands clasped decorously at the chest. Charlie Redmond drops an invisible set of rosary beads into his friend's palmed clasp, and he makes to speak, his own palms opened and displayed for sincerity. The manic warmth of his smile would light a chapel – Charlie's smile is, of its own right, an enlivened thing. It travels the terminal as though disembodied from him. It leaves a woven lace of hysterical menace in its wake.

A man of my seniority? he says. To be scrabbling trying to put the means of a living together? It's unnatural. I should be gone out to stud by now. I should be on a farm in fucken Wales.

He turns to Benny, to the dogs, to the sleeping girls.

Ye know that I don't have so much as a roof over my head? he says. I should be gone upriver by now. I should be gone westward into the sunset. I should be staring down at a wine-dark sea. I should have no more on my plate than issues of décor and light romantic entertainment. The way I'm thinking? A modern house looking over a moonlit bay. Sound familiar, Maurice? With underfloor heating. A washing machine that'd talk to you. Little dishwasher doing a jig in the corner. West Cork direction. Somewhere out beyond Berehaven, maybe?

Now he shoots up, dangerously, as though on a starter's pistol, and he spins about on the bad leg to ravish the imagined room of his retirement.

Open plan! he cries. I'm loving it! A sense of flow. Oh and these beautiful old floorboards! They've buffed up to a very nice finish! What's-her-face off Channel 4? Sarah Beeny. The makeover shows. Gorgeous. The floorboards warm under me bare feet. In the sunlight. Lovely kind of austerity about the whole look as well. There'll be nothing gaudy. I'm trying to get away from that side of myself. I was raised at the side of the fucken road. And the way the inside opens to the outside, with the reclaimed boards, the flow, the fields, the sea, the hills . . .

Charlie? Maurice says.

Sound familiar to you, Moss? A fine new house outside Berehaven? Laid out in it like the Lamb of God?

Leave it, Charles.

Why, Moss?

Sit down and take the weight off, boy. Relax yourself. You're getting the anxiety colour on you. The yellowy colour.

Charlie sits and drains the last dregs from a cava bottle.

I'm not saying we were down a coalmine, Maurice, he says. I'm not saying we were digging the roads. But there was a lot of work and a lot of travelling and there was a great deal of danger and annoyance. And Uncle Charlie, at his time of life, he needs to feel the proper reward of it.

I know, Charlie. I know.

They lean back together on the bench. Their eyes close in a soft, mysterious tandem. Benny, who has waited on his moment, manages to edge away from the men, unseen, and he takes the silent, prowling Lorca with him. Quickly he finds a policía.

It's about these men, he says.

The sleepy cop looks over but just smiles.

Those two? he says. Don't worry about them. They're always here.

*

A cold white moon speaks highly of the coming winter. The sea tonight has grown irritable. It guffs up a newsy froth. There is no word from the direction of Tangier. In the ferry terminal, wan beneath its lights, Maurice Hearne and Charlie Redmond stand as a vaudeville pair but the dreadlocked girls lie sleeping still – only the dog, Junior Cortés, is alive for the show.

We're down a man and a dog, Charlie.

Is the way that it goes.

If they were ever here at all.

They sit together on the bench. There is long-sufferance. There is woe. They are on a reminiscent drift again.

We were in a state back then, Maurice says.

This isn't news you're telling me, Charlie says.

The walls were melting. The clock was coming down the stairs. We were tremendously out of it almost all the time. I have big regrets. There were things I missed. There was a whole chunk of my life that passed me by. I don't remember 1997, Charles, and I'm not great on '98. Cynthia? She kept me going.

Cynthia, she could maintain.

Though I have every reason to believe that woman was the most deranged of us all.

Which is saying something, Maurice.

But oh Jesus, Charlie, at night, the fear that was on us.

Money brings up the fear, Moss.

There was so much money and we were pauperised half the time. How the fuck does that work? I mean you know how it was sometimes, Charlie. The way the money was flowing?

You remember that night in the house on Evergreen Street? We'd lost a tonne of prime Maroc?

Then we found it again. Outside Midleton.

We counted out so much fucken money on that couch. We were grinning like cats.

There was the night of the four Dutchmen in the boat.

Don't.

But the clock isn't going backwards, Charlie. Cynthia is dead and she's not coming back.

Leave it, Maurice. It's hard. We don't have to talk about it.

But Maurice Hearne falls to his knees in a gesture of hysterical collapse. He sighs out the long history of the stage. Leonor wakes and smiles at him.

Which one are you again?

Leonor.

Lovely name, Charlie, isn't it?

Gorgeous. Like an air freshener.

Have you seen this girl, have you? Photo's a bit old now,
but she might have the same kind of look to her still. Dilly
Hearne?

I haven't seen.

Why're ye all lying to us?

Maurice crawls on his fours across the floor and pants like a
dog at the girl's feet.

Jesus, she says.

Bit late in the day for him, Charlie says.

Tell us this, Leonor, seeing as you have the jaws working.
And just out of pure interest. But what's the nature of the
attraction? To this way of life ye've picked?

It's freedom, she says.

It's poverty, Charlie says. Poverty is always for free.

*

They sit until the night gives way to morning again. The
hard pure light of October 23rd is pushing through. Leonor
and Ana sit with their dog, Junior Cortés – the dog has a
rogue tongue, conspiratorial eyes. The girls and the dog
happily listen to the men, who have woven a ring around
them, a ring that shimmers, and it is made of these odd,
circling words.

I no longer love my body, says Maurice Hearne, thought-fully. I have no time for it.

I'm resigned to these old bones, says Charlie Redmond, shucking his cuffs.

I'm like a fucken ape, Maurice says. The long arms and the horrible, thick, solid kind of torso.

I crawl out of bed in the mornings, Charlie says, and I can barely hear myself for the groans.

I have the feeling in a perpetual way, Maurice says, that I'm in the next room across and I can't really hear myself at all.

You'd understand, Charlie says, darkening, how a spell can come over a man? When he hits on a certain age.

A spell? Ana says.

When he tips over the brink of fifty, Maurice says. That kind of direction.

They talk of ageing and death. They talk of those they have crossed and those they have helped, of their first loves and lost loves, of their enemies and friends. They talk of the old days in Cork, and in Barcelona, and in London, and in Málaga, and in the ghosted city of Cádiz. They talk of the feelings of those places. They talk about being here, once again, on the coast of Barbary, as though on a magnet's drag.

The likes of us have been drawn here for hundreds of years, Maurice says.

It's a straight run down the sea road, Charlie says.

As we look at them now indeed they seem to clarify: their smiles are high and piratical; their jauntiness has a cutlass edge.

You want to read up on the Riffians, Charlie says.

Coming off the Rif Mountains, Maurice says. Like a sack of snakes trying to deal with them people.

Their fathers' fathers' fathers? Charlie says. A couple of dozen of them would line up, with lanterns, on a high rise of the shore, and they'd string themselves out, and they'd lift and lower the lanterns in a sequence, rising and falling, slowly, in a rhythm, sweet as music . . .

Are ye watching it? Maurice says.

. . . so the effect, from the sea, was like a swaying boat. And that would draw another boat in, just to say hello, how's the fishing, only to get itself wrecked on the rocks, and here's the Riffians down with their lanterns and knives to finish the job.

That way of thinking, Maurice says, can only come from heavy use of the plant cannabis sativa.

The assassin's plant, Charlie says.

The black oily Riffian hashish, Maurice says. Oh, you'd think you'd died and gone to heaven altogether. And do ye realise, by the way, that ye're lookin' at a man here beside me who's opened throats himself?

And the pirate Charlie Redmond leans back on the bench with a diamond grin.

*

But the money no longer is in dope. The money now is in people. The Mediterranean is a sea of slaves. The years have turned and left Maurice and Charlie behind. The men are elegiacal, woeful, heavy in the bones. Also they are broke and grieving. Ana rises up in the shape of a yawn. She stretches out to the full, airy capacities of being twenty-three. She is happy to see the new day light the high windows. She reaches for Junior Cortés. The dog moves in to nuzzle her sweetly about the groin.

That dog knows which end is the sleeves, Charlie says.

Can't be taught, Maurice says.

Ana scowls at Charlie and squats on the bench and looks Maurice hard in the eye and she says –

Perroflauta.

I beg your pardon?

The Spanish for crusty, she says, is perroflauta.

It means a-dog-and-a-flute, Leonor says.

We're away in a hack, Charlie says.

Perro . . . flauta, Maurice tries the word, softly, in wonder.

They say it as a curse, Leonor says.

Because they don't like us, Ana says. They say we're dirty. They don't want the camps. They don't want no dogs. That's why we go to Maroc.

And who looks after Junior Cortés?

People come back. We go out. We share the dogs. We can't bring the dogs across.

Confirmation, Charlie says.

Ye have people due in from Tangier?

Maybe.

It depends on the boats.

And if the men are to see the girl Dilly again, they know that it depends also on fate's arrangements, and on the drifting insistences of youth. Leonor and Ana turn to whisper to each other now and laugh quietly and they stand up and gather their things – they have no fear of these men.

Thanks for the drinks, Ana says.

At least tell us more about this witchin', Charlie says.

I actually have long experience of witches, Maurice says.

They were drawn to you, Moss, always, the witchy types.

Did you know you use green wood to burn a witch, Charlie?

There's sense to it. Somehow.

Spells? Curses? Maurice says. Oh, I been involved with the whole lot of it. Can ye do a spell for me, ladies?

Who do you want to put a spell on? Leonor says.

Have you a biro? Maurice says. We can start making a list.

What you do, Leonor says, is you take a piece of cloth. Maybe from some old clothes of the person you want to reach. And you put things inside.

Kind of things?

Hairs . . . from down here?

Pubes?

And the finger . . . piece?

Fingernail?

Fingernails. Pu-bez. And dry blood on maybe the tampon.

What kind of people are ye at all? Charlie says.

Also, Ana says. In the cloth. A chemical.

It's called antimony, Leonor says.

You think there's a spell can bring my daughter back?

She's a small girl.

She's a pretty girl.

She was in Granada maybe?

And not long ago.

Dill? Or Dilly? It comes from Dilys.

Chapter Four

LOVERS AT THE
NORTH GATE

*In the city of Cork, and in the Maam Valley, and in
Barcelona, and in London, and in the town of
Berehaven, from March 1994 to April 1999*

He believed that the flat was being watched. Mostly he
did not sleep at all. What they'd had shipped from Málaga
had briefly suppressed the town's anxieties. Also it had
angered its older wolves. We have climbed too quickly
above our station. He spoke to Karima from the coin
phone on the haunted stairwell of the old house at St
Luke's Cross. There would be a shipment again soon. He
was lying in the bed with lumps of money on the floor
beside him. Cynthia turned in her sleep and spoke from
the far deeps of dread. Her thin haunch was candle pale.
They would break into the flat and leave him for dead and
take the money. They would batter her senseless or worse.
Charlie Redmond was already in hiding in the west of the
county. Maurice looked out from their eyrie above the city,

weak from sleeplessness, and the smoke that rose from the river in the late-winter morning was dense and ominous.

*

As the day came up to the meagre light it possessed, Maurice and Cynthia went out to walk for a while. They had fallen in love in the usual goofy ways. The taste of her black hair. The static that lifted from her. Even the air was excitable around her. They went out to walk in the cold by the river. Their voices fell into conspiracy above the river's voices. By the North Gate they went – with her hand in his – and across the shaky bridge and out through the waking town. It was so cold you could see the dogs' barks on the air. They were like waifs out by the river. Out here, it was as if the world had backed off from them for a spell. They believed in fatedness and meant-to-be's. They believed in the dark star that was theirs to steer by.

She had a way of talking that made him realise he would not find a way out. She let him know there was no way to escape from himself. She could see what was coming.

*

They went to hide in the Maam Valley. He believed the wolves were in pursuit. The wolves wore zip-up tops and Fila trainers. Maurice and Cynthia learned to drive out there. It was comic and strange to be living in the country. It was the last hard bones of the winter, but the evenings were stretching a little and the roads after rain were black sliding tongues and gleamed. Their landlord, John James McGann, of Clifden, gave them the run of a battered Ford Fiesta. It wore neither tax nor insurance. There was a smell

of sweet drink off McGann, a sherry. There was a papery
film like mothskin stretched over his eyes. He slithered
about making goldfish gasps as though traumatised by an
otherworld invisible but to his eyes. He wore a corduroy
suit in a marmalade shade. He was a cattish sort and
slow-gesturing. Maurice and John James could hear each
other's thinking. They talked about money. John James felt
like a super-strange mentor type. The rented cottage was at
a height above Loch an Oileáin. The lake was pitch and
eerie. There was a tiny lake island that sat there oddly, as
though unsure of its purpose in the greater scheme. Above,
the Maumturks were the most sober mountains. The
Maumturks had slow, blank, unobliging faces. Maurice and
Cynthia loved each other out there.

The days were cold as evil but the evenings spread magic
from the sea inwards and stretched out and tapped the place
until it was open to our dreaming.

*

He really fucking liked her hands. In the narrow bed in
the cottage they whispered and tunnelled together to the
bottom of the night and lay there dazed and happy
afterwards.

We're after making pigs of ourselves again, she said.

*

He liked too that the house was at a height. He could see
what was coming up the road at them. That there was no
phone was ideal. He called his mother from the pub in
Maam Cross and told her they were in Barcelona.

It sounds lively, she said.

The shipment arranged through Karima had made him one hundred and seven thousand Irish pounds. An equal share was gone to Charlie Redmond. Cynthia phoned her father from the pub in Maam Cross and said they were in London and going to India for a while.

I think you should put Maurice on the phone to me, her father said, and she hung up.

From the pub in Maam Cross he phoned Charlie, too, who told him the weather in the south was changeable. It was best to stay hidden for a while.

He suffered night sweats, heart rattles, bouts of raving. She knelt above him in the bed and hushed him and told him that she loved him. He told her that once, as a young man, his father got so bad he had to be strapped down to a bed in Berehaven.

It's just the fear of it, she said.

The fear of turning into our parents, she said, is what turns us into our fucking parents.

She was not wrong – the mind designs the body.

*

And then for a while they fell into the quietude of the place. Always, as the years passed, they would name it as the best time in their lives. When we had mountain and when we had water.

Let it be a drowsy time, she said, and turned slowly a white haunch to him.

She told him that the money couldn't be left just as money. It had to work for itself. They tried to drive in the evenings as the hours of daylight pushed back against the dark.

A, b, c, he said. Accelerator, brake, clutch.

I'm not a fucking halfwit, she said.

The ditches sang in the evening light, the birds. She drove at twenty miles an hour down a back road outside Maam Cross. Small birds were flung up from the ditches.

Do you hear a cuckoo?

Watch the fucken road, Cyn. We'll end up in the field.

She was beautiful as she drove – the worms of concentration wriggled on her brow. She said the most important thing was to maintain a distance from Charlie Redmond.

*

He dropped the rent into McGann in Clifden on Wednesdays. He was out of an old story from somewhere – country auctioneer with a sherried nose. Always he quizzed his tenant oddly.

Any stirrings on that island, Maurice? On the lake?

Nothing to report, Mr McGann.

Keep your eye on the island, I'd say. That place could have news for you. One of the nights.

61

He talked with the strange old man about the rain and the sea, the boats that were out, the thinness of the ground in places around here. They talked about houses and the price of land.

It'd be a time to buy, McGann said.

Me buying houses?

What else would you be doing with your money?

*

Whenever he looked down on the lake, he knew that bodies had been hidden on the island there. Maybe not in the recent past. They got braver in the Fiesta by quick leaps. She began to talk nightly in bed about cities, life, people. They were too young for the Maam Valley. The idyll was ending and then May was on the doorstep and he bought the cottage from John James McGann for forty thousand pounds. By the end of the month they had it let for the summer entirely and they went to live in Barcelona.

*

They fucked each other with fierceness. She spat and bit and swore. He said crazy fucking things. The strip of blue, blue sky visible in the crack between the curtains; his hand between her legs. The cusp and clatch, the tender sips, and we have nothing to do all day, Cynthia, and nothing that wants doing anyway.

*

They walked in the afternoons through the Barri Gòtic. On ancient narrow streets the gargoyles lurched, the fountains whispered. They tried on clothes in scuzzy boutiques. They listened to house music sent on cassettes from Cork and to The Pixies but only the first three LPs. A shipment that set out from Ceuta was taken in on a clear night by Eyeries on the coast of the Beara Peninsula and realised another eighty thousand pounds. She wondered if Charlie could not be cut out at this point.

On a rainy day, at the back of an arcade on Carrer de la Portaferrissa, they were tattooed – each atop the left breast took a tiny '13'.

*

At the zinc counter of a bar known for its anchovies, in Plaça de la Vila de Gràcia, in the district of Gràcia, Maurice spoke calmly, for more than an hour, over small glasses of Estrella Damm beer, as he attempted to ease the nerves of Charlie Redmond, who had two days previously left a man for dead in Deptford.

Trouble finds me, Charlie said, and a stray tear rolled down his sentimental cheek. I don't go looking for it, Maurice. It come knocking for me. Trouble. With a big ignorant face on him.

You'll be fine a while here.

Fine? You haven't seen what I left behind me on that toilet fucken floor on Barfleur Lane.

Charlie's shoulders rolled with injustice. Cynthia did not want him within a thousand miles.

We could set you up in Málaga, Maurice said.

You runnin' me from the place already?

There was a ragged boy with a flute and an old dog on a rope in the square outside, and as the boy blew tunelessly on the flute and sang some words to his old sick dog, as the broken notes rose up, Maurice came out of his skin, and he could see the scene from above, and the square was taking on the deeper tones of evening – hushed and velvet notes – and now Cynthia moved briskly across the square.

She entered the café and he was in his body again. She hugged and kissed Charlie on the cheek. She made eyes to Maurice over Charlie's shoulder – get him the fuck out of here. But it was safer to have Charlie Red close in.

*

The streets of Gràcia were in the slow hours of the afternoon almost deserted. He rang his mother from the payphone in the square.

There was a man come looking for you, Moss, she said. And as quare-lookin' a hawk as ever stood up in a suit.

A suit?

Suited and booted, she said. Any amount of a turn-out.

He realised that she knew everything.

I said nothing, Maurice. I stood there and acted the fool. And our friend, he just looks at me, with the little smile on him, and he says . . . 'Is he still in Spain, missus?'

Cynthia said –

When we leave a place, we buy a place. We keep an interest.

The next day he put a deposit on a bar in L'Eixample. They knew that the city would go up. They walked through it in the evenings. They kept away from the Barri Xinès because heroin sang from its every doorway. They employed a masochist called Laura from Sitges to take over the running of the bar in the evenings. She drew a masochist crowd and soon the takings had doubled.

But what are we going to do with ourselves, Maurice?

Well, this is it. The old question.

I mean who the fuck are we?

Oh, we're a very old type, he said. We're merchant traders.

*

The vicinity of Stroud Green. The bones of London. The light was weak and apologetic. Dilly, in the bouncer, was eerily silent, wide-eyed. Cynthia was away to have an hour. There was a white van parked out there all day. Half-a-smile was granted from the elf in the bouncer – my heartbreaker. Maurice smoked a little weed out the window. Charlie Redmond was now in hiding in the Maam Valley. It was all gone to Jesus. Apart from the money, because the money was fabulous.

And here she came, outside, with the long face on. Harder to read lately. The winter had smashed them.

She took the joint from his hand. She drew on it grimly. The cold of the day was on her cheeks. February is a godawful month just about everywhere. She'd gone skinnier since the child. He wanted to be back in Spain. Pigeon-grey, fag-ash grey, clay-of-the-graveyard London. The great fear, the vast unspoken – was it drugs in the months of the pregnancy had the child staring up out of the bouncer like a fucking zombie?

Also, his mother was threatening a visit. You'd put yourself under a fucking lorry altogether. The dim thunder of the evening trains. The face on Cynthia – was there something to read there? What now, what next? She was tired and wan; she was pulled this way and the other. The smoke was shared between them.

There's a van down the road, Maurice.

The white one?

It was there an hour ago and it's still there now. Two men sat in it. Big fuckers.

He shook his head and took up the child – Dilly kicked out her feet in tiny electric jolts to the full stretch of the Babygro.

It's nothing.

There are two men. In a van. Down the fucking road, Maurice.

And soon it will be dark again – the lights of all the cages came on against the February evening.

You think they'd just announce themselves?

She blew a dense, greenish smoke out the gap in the window.

The fuck do I know?

He stood on the couch to see down the road. Baby moo-moo in his arms still. Like a fox with its nose in the air. Protect the cub.

Just before the hackney base, she said.

Will I swing past?

Do not go out that fucking door, Maurice.

She double-bolted the front door. He put the child in the bouncer again. He licked the papers for a joint.

They could be checking the meters, he said. They could be TV licence.

What fucking meters?

They could be Haringey Council.

The street was quiet most of the day and night. It had a sullen or a watchful air. The baby began softly to cry. He took her up again and brought her to the kitchen and ran the tap. He looked to the long back garden that ran to the steep embankment, the railway line. A train roared into view. Silent faces were lit on the evening train. How the foxes screamed at night. Dilly's sobbing faded as the tap water circled the sinkhole. She twitched silently in his arms with contentment.

They're out of the van, Maurice!

And two big fucking Spanish heads on them.

Shoulders the breadth of Madrid.

They leaned back against the van and smoked fervently –
they looked down towards the house with calm.

He wrapped the child warm in her bundling.

Cynthia threw things in a bag, wallets, cards.

They went out the back garden – they hid silently in the
cold, lifeless February garden.

Night already was falling.

They hid in the garden until it was fully dark.

They edged down the embankment to the track.

They walked terrified in its lee.

The gravel swam under their feet.

Small mammals scurried.

Night-time across Haringey, Crouch End, Stroud Green.

Breathing silently the great maw of Finsbury Park.

Pulsing the mainline vein of the Seven Sisters.

They stayed a sleepless night at a guesthouse in Crouch
End. The night aged slowly as a decade. Maurice was as old
now as he'd ever felt, but yes, there was Dilly, who was

silent and gorgeous and yes, definitely, he was in love with her. It was time to go back to Ireland.

Sea-rock; salt-wind; home.

*

From above the town of Berehaven its harbour was streaked with knives of cold blue in the April sun. Dilly made a tuneless song on her lips as her eyes followed an early butterfly, the flicker of a whitish yellow as light as her breath. Dilly had a skin delicate and ash-pale, and the builder, Murphy, considered the child, smiling.

This one's away on her own little planet, he said.

Tell me about it, Maurice said.

The child's hand was clammy in his. He rubbed his thumb softly against the slick of her palm – this was a reassurance somehow. The three of them walked the raw acres of the site. It was set on a plateau in the stone hills above town. There was a weird mound with a few bushes at one end. The plan was for a crescent of houses. The swathe of a half-moon would be arranged to keep the wind off from the west.

Are there a few trees we could put around back?

Well, Murphy said.

Is there nothing will take?

The ground's fucken rock, Murphy said. There's nothing pretty will take.

There would be a view at least. Maurice lifted the child into his arms and made groans of protest at her weight. In truth, at three and a half years old, she was pixie weight. He pointed south to the opening world.

Some view, Dill?

He drew her eye across the rooftops of the town, over the masts and scrabble of the harbour, to Bere Island beyond.

Island View Terrace? Maurice said.

Harbour View? Murphy tried.

Or something Irishy?

Now, Murphy agreed.

How're you fixed for the Irish, Dilly?

The child grinned at him shyly.

Something about croí, Maurice said. Isn't croí the heart?

Croí briste, Murphy said, and they laughed.

Heartbreak Ridge, Maurice said. Fucken right, with that wind in on top of you.

Murphy kicked at the ground sadly.

Tell you this much, he said. Me croí will be fucken briste and I trying to put foundations in that.

When'll we get a start?

Depends on a few things.

Such as?

He was sorry that he asked. It concerned the circular mound, the whitethorn bushes. He pulled the zip of Dilly's anorak to the neck against the wind. He brushed her cold cheek with his fingertips. Her mother's precise frown was set on her lips. Everything was in place already.

They're going to be skinned up here, Dill, he said, if we don't get a few trees down.

The builder Murphy seemed to take this as personal affront. His brow darkened; he considered sullenly his Caterpillar boots.

It's the West of Ireland, he said. There's a tendency to fucken wind.

*

He walked with Dilly through the square in Berehaven. On the dock he bought turbot and a few queenies, some samphire. He promised the child there would be no more mackerel, and she made a happy face.

We'll go for our drinks, Dill? Find your mother.

He was on a slow taper but he had an hour yet. You could drink against it. The pub was heaving at mid-morning. Little wonder the country was gone the way it was gone. A trawler flush with octopus had waddled into port. The crew was in the West End Bar bursting the ball on itself. By the crate the Corona went down, and the vodka Red Bull, and

71

they were roaring out of them – they fell about unpleasantly on sea legs. Holy Thursday. The last year of the century. He arranged Dilly on a high stool and poured her orange drink over ice.

Your mother will ate me for the Fanta, he said.

A few beached-up Spanish lads sipped woefully at long-neck bottles to turn the West End into a grim cervecería. Galician probably. Very Irish there. Melancholia, all the rest of it. Redheads. The last was seen of him he was after fucking himself into the Bay of Biscay. Often it was Spanish-feeling this season in Berehaven.

The bar girl hovered into view with her lip stud gleaming and leaned to Maurice across the counter –

How ye gettin' on above? she said.

Topping, he said.

He felt a stab of desire for her but it might pass. Cynthia arrived in as vaguely as a rumour of the place. Her eyes were warm on the needle's tip. She kissed the top of the child's head and was regarded with dour puzzlement. They were at a remove from everybody else. The questions already had been raised – is it houses ye're building up there? And the planning came through?

Is there something wrong with the place? Cynthia said.

How'd you mean?

What's wrong with the fucking site, Maurice?

It's windy. It's a peninsula.

The Spanish were hunched in a religious aspect. As if summoning the Infant. The octopus crew bawled and grew narkier. They clutched at each other erotically. They twanged each other's underpants. A thin horizontal of the town square was visible beneath the blind. A holiday SUV coasted to a halt and disgorged a unit of fat kids. The little bastards had the country ate alive. An old man with a smell of fields and disinfectant sidled in beside them.

Only the Russians, he said.

I'm sorry?

Only the cunten Russians, he said, have less class than us when they get a few pound.

The pub light was a brownish gold and forgiving. Cynthia looked fine in it and the child was beautiful.

The bones is gone so bad now, the old man said, it's a class of horse ointment I'm smearin' into meself. How're ye getting on with the place above?

Flying it, Cynthia said.

Early days, Maurice said.

How many houses?

It's all being worked out, Cynthia said.

We'll keep you posted, Maurice said.

The need had taken hold. Soon he would have to take the pain from the day. He arranged the clock of his day precisely. He would shoot up at one or at ten past in the back bedroom. Cynthia was already looked after. They had worked out between them a schedule adapted for the child.

*

They had rented an unfurnished house in a fold of the Caha Mountains. They watched the night move across the moonscape of the peninsula. Dilly turned in a hot bundle in the back room and spoke indecipherably among her dreams. Cynthia and Maurice sat on deckchairs by the naked fire grate. The air was still tonight, and mild. They drank Spanish wine and smoked charas. There would be no heroin until morning. There was such a thing as discipline. She searched him out about the site again and finally he confessed.

There is some bollocks, he said, about a fairy fort up there.

With a swirl of the wrist she moved the inky rioja. They smiled at each other.

You know the kind of moundy bit down the far end? he said.

I do, yeah, she said.

Raised earth in a circular run, a scraggle of whitethorn bushes around it – the child always had a moonful look when she played there.

You've kept quiet about this.

It's bollocks, Cynthia.

It's Murphy is saying this?

He says some of his lads mightn't build there. The blockies, at least.

You were going to tell me this when?

It's nonsense.

The men won't build on a site we've paid four hundred and eighty-five thousand pounds for because they think there's a fairy fort up there. And you felt this was beyond remark?

Fairy fort is stretching it, he said. It's just these superstitions you get locally. About places. It's the moundy bit on the far side. Apparently it has all the characteristics of a fairy fort.

And since when the fuck, Maurice, would you know the characteristics of a fairy fort?

There's such a thing as the fucken internet, he said.

Dilly was found to be more soundly sleeping. They dialled up the internet – it made noises of strangulation as it at slow length connected. They drank rioja and examined images of fairy forts.

This is kind of . . .

It's kind of precisely what we've paid five hundred grand for.

Four eight five, he said.

It was not good to dig into the apocrypha. Builders who had no more than cleared the brush from these sites had gone down to sudden collapses, galloping tumours. Motorway schemes had been diverted.

They took down a bottle of whiskey. The price had seemed generous for the view of harbour and mountains, for the extent of the acreage. They lit a few sticks in the fire and drank whiskey and spoke of what they had read; they spoke of raths and forts and liosanna. There was strange glamour as they remembered these old words on their lips.

*

Now they became obsessed with the idea that they had fallen into bad luck. They took heroin against the idea. The measured quantities that had distinguished their previous habits as models of noble restraint went out the fucking window. Now they were horsing into it. And the aura of bad luck was at once everywhere. It was around them like a nervous village. The stone hills spoke out the rumour of the bad luck. The wind blew the rumour in swirls about their feet. Bad luck, bad luck – the idea entertained itself, fattened, came to fruition. They took cocaine in breakneck quantities against the idea of the bad luck. They were hammering into the Powers, the John Jameson, it was breakfast from the bottle and elevenses off the mirror. The child would as well be raised by the cats that sat lazily in what April sun troubled itself to come across the rooftops of Berehaven. The build was a disaster from the get-go. A young fella from Sneem, as broad as he was long, broke his leg on the first morning of construction. Word of the accident was around the fishwives of

Berehaven like a fast fucking fire. Up on the wind-blown site, there was a sense that morning of fatalism, unhinged-ness, morbid introspection. Day two some fucking eejit with a kango hammer nearly took the marriage prospects off himself. Day five a thirty-two-year-old man from Glengarriff had a mini-stroke while he was mixing bags of sand and gravel. The builder Murphy was by now having trouble keeping his numbers up, and he was depressed and drinking heavily the length of the slow evenings in the West End Bar. Maurice drove into Cork city on Thursday mornings to meet the first Dublin train on which was ferried their week's supply of heroin. The tenth morning of the build – a Friday – they were aware that the week's supply had been badly cut and were raging about it, and just then Charlie Redmond phoned from Spain to say a speedboat containing a half-tonne of their Moroccan hashish had been taken by the Guardia Civil just as it came into La Línea de la Concepción. Bad luck, bad luck. The boat had been spotted at Ceuta, it seemed, but what were you going to do? Charlie Redmond was affecting a note of blithe indifference which Maurice Hearne was in no fucking form for. Putting foundations in the rocks of the hills above Berehaven was dreadful work. The rocks screamed and whined dangerously as they were drilled into. The children of the rocks cried out. We are making marks here that we have no right to make. We'll answer for it. Bad luck, bad luck. He was starting to wonder if Cynthia had a thing for the builder Murphy, who was a big hand-some uncouth motherfucker, but with dainty touches for the ladies, and his black depression perhaps lent a poetical air. Maurice drove alone above the site and looked down on the construction and masturbated sorrowfully about the girl who worked in the West End Bar in the afternoons. With Cynthia he mixed the cut heroin with cocaine to make speedballs, and they shot them up and fucked each other and then they'd have a fight after it. Bad luck, bad luck. The guards were driving past the site daily with interested little smiles. Another labourer spat blood copiously the first morning of the third week as the trench of foundations edged towards the fairy mound and he was never seen again. Half the builders on site by now were Spanish fishermen beached off the trawlers and good for nothing as they were lacerated by the weather. It had turned into a wet April and it was so cold in the sea-damp and Maurice Hearne was hearing old voices in the night. But they stuck at it. There was such a thing as bullheadedness. The houses started to break out across the hill – a crescent of nine houses to be named Ard na Croí. A boatload of cocaine worth two million pounds was taken a few miles down the coast, and Maurice was brought in and questioned. It was a Wednesday night. That he knew nothing was soon evident. As he left the stationhouse, the detective said – you'll want an early start in the morning, Moss, get in and meet that Dublin train. He wanted to leave the place again but was rooted to it now. Fucking Ireland. Its smiling fiends. Its speaking rocks. Its haunted fields. Its sea memory. Its wildness and strife. Its haunt of melancholy. The way that it closes in.

Chapter Five

MOTHER FIST AND HER FIVE DAUGHTERS

At the port of Algeciras, in October 2018

Time runs on odd bends here. There are days and nights you wouldn't know where the fuck you are nor when. The people come and go. Their eternal faces; their lips moving silently across the seven distractions. Soon, again, the boats will come and go. When we move by water, our hearts are moved. We are complicated fucking machines. Now the hours melt one into the other at the port of Algeciras. For the fading Irish gangsters the long wait continues –

You know what I get to wondering, Maurice?

Tell me, Charlie.

About death, Moss.

Here we go.

Is it as raw a deal as they make it out to be?

Come again?

Is it not in some way an ease when she comes calling? The
Black Angel? . . . Hush now . . . Listen? . . . The gentle
flapping of her wings . . . You hearing it?

Charles?

Are we as well off out of it, Maurice? Is what I'm asking.
With all the bollock-acting that do be going on?

I'm not seeing a picnic coming, Charlie. Death-wise.

You think it's the end?

I'm not saying it's the end. I'm just not seeing a picnic.

I have a happy enough view of the Big D. So happens.

What are you seeing down there, Charlie? At the end of
the road?

I'm not seeing a meadow full of flowers. I'm not saying that
for one minute. Not seeing a moonful bay neither. With all
your old birds there, and they lined up, waiting on you, one
after the other, in the peach of their youths. Their rosy
cheeks and their glad little eyes. I'm not seeing that by any
means. But what I am imagining, Maurice, is a kind of . . .
quiet. You know? Just a kind of . . . silence.

Lovely, Maurice Hearne says. Restful.

When you think what we put up with in our lives?
Noise-wise?

It's a cacophony, Mr Redmond.

We come into the world on the tip of a scream and the wave of our poor mothers' roaring.

Our poor mams with the straw nearly ripped out of the mattresses.

And the first thing we do? We start roaring and bawling our own selves. We open the lungs and let rip. We give it what-for. And how do we go out? At the far end of life? Often enough in the same way. Roaring out of us!

And what goes on in between?

Noise, Maurice. Nothing but noise and consternation.

You look for the quiet spaces in a life, Charles. And do you find them?

In your hole you do.

Or in love, maybe.

Maybe so.

I loved her, Charlie.

I know that. I'm very sorry.

For a long while. I knew her, you know? Cynthia. I knew who she was.

Do you think about where she's gone to now?

I do, yeah. I'm not seeing a picnic, Charlie.

You mean, what if it's just . . .

More of it.

On the far side. What's if it's just . . .

Noise?

*

A ferry boat lands in from Tangier. There is activity again across the Straits. A few ragged youths saunter drowsily across the terminal floor. They have the weight of Africa on their backs. They are watched with bead of eye by the mildly natty, mildly decrepit Irishmen.

Dilly Hearne?

Dill or Dilly?

She's a small girl.

She's a pretty girl.

Dreadlocks. Dog-on-a-rope type. That kind of an aul' gaatch to her.

The men sit restlessly on the bench. They are at a high vantage atop the stack of their years. They are old enough for the long view in either direction now.

It got tricky, Maurice says. With Dilly. As she got older. By the time she was fourteen or fifteen? Slugging around the place with a leper face on. And the school she was at? The place really annoyed me, actually.

The Sisters of Perpetual . . .

Whatever they fucken were. I remember one day, Charles, at the height of it, a day when I seriously had other things on my plate. But it was irking me, you know? The idea of poor Dill at that school. So I got on the blower to the principal. I gave her an absolute leathering. I said listen now, missus, okay? I'm not saying I'm in charge of the uniforms at all. But do ye not realise what ye're dealing with here? These are very open young people. They're still being formed. These are young girls fifteen years of age. And the way ye make them go around the place in those horrible old uniforms? Awful shapeless skirts and jumpers, down to their ankles, like sacks on them. Ye're trying to make these girls deny themselves! And they're beautiful girls! You know what it is? It's Catholic fucken hijab!

That was telling her, Maurice.

I'm not saying I was in any position to be getting up on my high horse. At the moment of speaking I was a mile off the coast of Clare with a half-tonne of Moroccan hashish in the hold. And the fear of screeching Jesus on me. And the water rolling and the boat listing . . . God help me . . . Pitching and rolling a mile out from Fanore . . . A morning of the winter, and there's no sign of Charlie Redmond, nor his fucken lorry . . . And I'm thinking, Maurice? You're too long in the tooth now for this lark . . . I was thinking, my daughter is the important thing now, she should be my . . . my focus, you know?

You made a fabulous dad, Maurice. In my opinion.

But then the mist kind of parted . . . And there were two headlamps . . . Burning . . . Just there . . . In the grey

83

morning . . . Above the old pier, at Fanore . . . And there he was, Charlie Redmond, of Farranree . . . Like a man that would never let you down.

*

You think there's an end in sight, Charlie?

Boats come in, the boats go out. She could make an appearance yet.

But what I get to wondering?

Don't, Moss.

Is it pretty girls make graves?

We'd know. Somehow. At a gut level. If she weren't drawing the wind no more.

You think she's after hawkin' us over?

It's in her blood to be hawkin' us. Her mother was the same way. Crooked as the day.

And a tongue on her, Cynthia. When I came back without the eye on me? From Tangier? She took one look, after all I'd suffered, and she said who the fuck do you think you are, Thom Yorke?

Never heard of him. Or hang about . . . He wasn't a lame boy from Summerhill?

He's the lad out of Radiohead, Charlie.

Never liked them. Whining bastards. And the amount of

money the cunts are making? They should have the ukuleles out.

He have the one eye guzz on him.

Making any amount of money. And he whining out of him like a stuck goat? Should have his mambas out.

Do you think it made me handsomer, Charlie? In a peculiar way? The fucked-up eye?

It gave you a bit of character, Moss.

Sayin' I had none beforehand?

You were bland-enough looking as a younger gent, Maurice, in fairness.

You'd say that for it. The ageing. It does give you a bit of sauce. In a peculiar way.

It's the desperation make us saucy. Gents of a certain age. But as a matter of fact, Moss? For all the groaning out of us? For all we'd be whinging away like we're stuck in the middle of Radiohead of a wet Tuesday? The fact is we're in our prime. You and me? We're three o'clock of a summer's afternoon.

Hard to enjoy it, Charlie. I have an amount of guilt. Still.

Of course you have. On account of you nearly killed the girl.

Difficult to go there. Even yet.

I know, Maurice. I'm sorry.

*

From beneath the stones of the Algeciras dockside the humid air of reminiscence rises – it is one of the places of the earth designed for a good wallow.

My father?

Charlie Redmond smiles but sombrely. He looks to the high windows. He shakes his head in wonderment.

I reckon my father was the palest man in Cork city, he says.

Which is saying fucken something, Maurice says.

He should have been a priest. He shouldn't have spawned at all. It would have saved the world a whole heap of both-eration. He believed in God and humble destinies. He believed this was but the Vale of Tears. We were only passing through.

He might have been on the money there, Charlie.

Retired of a Friday. Took a massive stroke the following Tuesday. Sixty-five years of age. He gets himself planted in the wet clay. A man that was never late for work a day in his life.

Old bones. Going by the like of my poor dad's reach.

Those were hard times for you, Maurice. What were you? Eighteen? Nineteen?

It was after we moved to the new flat. College Road. By St Fin Barre's. He wasn't right in himself. He'd sit in a deck-chair out at the front door and play Hank Williams records. The Hank was never a good sign. It was summer and it'd be

86

nearly bright at eleven o'clock still. He's in his deckchair. The mother bringing him out cups of strong tea. Hank is going for it on the Sanyo Music Centre. The mother operated on the principle that strong tea was your only man for nerves. The father was gone from the job by that stage. He was gone from the port of Cork.

When the work is done for? Charlie says. Throw a stick at it.

He was on the Disability. He wouldn't sleep so much as a flea. He was in touch with odd elements, Charlie. I totally fucken believe this. He was like . . . a receiver. For strange fucken transmissions. The mother parading out to him with the sad little face and the mug of strong tea. Hank giving it plenty of the lonesome. Drinkers coming out of the Abbey Tavern across the road. Not a bother on them. Height of summer, bright at eleven bells, and my mother would be watching for the draw. We won't know it now, she'd say, until there's an old draw in the evenings, it'll be closing in on top of us. For a poor man depressed as bejesus since the day he first peeped out, to have to be listening to that? But he knew well enough that lacking her he'd be sucking his thumbs in a locked room.

Marriage, Charlie says. Beautiful and cruel.

Freaking out about me kept them going. I was a blessing. The freaking out gave them an interest in life. Maurice is going to wind up in Cork jail. What'll he do, Noel? He might go to England. He'd be as well off, Noelie? Elsewise they'll have a cot warmed for him in Cork jail, Ciss. My father. In his deckchair, at midnight, and Hank Williams Senior is wailing blue misery.

And Maurice can see it very clearly, even still, the summer night is pale, the late drinkers are still straggling from the Abbey, and his father is at the door, in his stripy deckchair, coming to his end, and bats at midnight thrill the cathedral eaves.

I think we had a heart-to-heart twice ever in our lives. Myself and the father. One time? It was that first winter on College Road. We were sat in front of the telly, Sunday afternoon, a football match, Highbury, it's a December Sunday.

Rags of snow on the pitch. The players blue under the winter lights. Sunday afternoon at the flats – the waft of roasted meats, and kids all over the shop, bawling.

He looks at me, Charlie. Says, what are you going to do with yourself, Moss? And I could tell then that he was going, I could tell he was on the road home. I don't know really, Da, I said. I might go to England yet.

It was Arsenal versus United. Bad-tempered and sparky. His father leaned forward and pulled up his socks. They watched the game steadily and they were careful not to look at each other.

You might be as well off, Moss, he said. Not saying England would be easy. It's not easy there at all. Did I ever tell you about a rough turn I took in Wolverhampton? I mean before I met your mother even. Wolverhampton was bleak, Moss. The blacks were eating dog food. I took a bad turn. I didn't know which end was up.

The light outside was pinched and mean at half past three. The familiar voice of the commentator soothed the afternoon like a drug. The world pressed in tightly on all sides but in simultaneous motion it opened out – this was a kind of breathing – and Maurice Hearne was nineteen years old. Out of nowhere and the London sky a wonder goal occurred at Highbury – it was a flying volley, an *educated* volley, from thirty yards. His father, without thinking, rose to his feet and applauded. Maurice smiled but he did not like the look of this move one bit. His father sat down again with a grimace. Maurice was already watchful of his own moods and changes, and he knew that this was not in itself a good sign. A tang of sibling absence inside was something not quite available to words. Out of nowhere and the winter sky came a statement from his father that cut to the muscle of the thing –

You're not like my crowd at all, Maurice. You're like her crowd.

He recognised the generosity in it, and the reassurance – he did not buy them.

And you're nearly as well off, Moss.

A few weeks later, Charlie? We hadn't seen Christmas out and the man was on a locked ward again.

Harsh, Maurice.

Smoke-grey bricks. Relic of Victoriana. The Bughouse. The green corridor that held three centuries' pain and misery as deep. Maurice wasn't allowed onto the ward itself. He was led to a visitors' room that felt like an interrogation unit. The dampness and the peel; the intense hatred of civic Ireland. He waited and smoked. After a while a heavy male nurse brought his father in, shuffling. His father wept at the sight of Maurice. He was cut with small nicks where they had imprecisely shaved him.

Ah, stop that, Da, would you?

He reached across the table and made to touch his father's arm – Jesus fuck – but something caused him to desist.

(Something? The land, the air, the sky; our church, our sea, our blood.)

Who the fuck's after giving you them slippers?

Bigfoot, his father said.

The nurse brought a mug of tea and custard creams for his father. He ate them cheerlessly and quick, as though it were a penance, and the tea was gone in a few big farmer slurps. He was a country boy with his wires twisted all wrong. He should have never been let near a city.

Mam'll be out to you tonight, I'd say.

There was an enormous clock on the wall and it slowed the moments remorselessly. He could ask his father how it had been for him but something would not allow it. He felt no fear as he looked across the table at the bombstruck man. His father had heard all the consternation of the heavens and he was still able to suck down custard creams.

Are you getting any sleep, Da?

Ah, I am, yeah.

I don't think you need to be worried about me ever, Da. You know that, don't you?

His father could not speak but nodded.

I wouldn't be able for this, Maurice said. You're stronger.

He walked back along the corridor with his father and the nurse. The afternoon traffic of the corridor. These poor blasted men in their stained pyjamas. The weepers and the chucklers. The moon-pale arses hanging out the back ends of them. The Martian glances. Whoever was shaving the poor fuckers had a sensational dose of the shakes.

His father opened his wrists in the bath two days after he got out. He left a note cellotaped to the bathroom door to the effect that she should not enter. Call 999.

And that's the way it goes, Charlie.

First they takes your money, then they takes your clothes.

*

The boats have been queued and now another arrives in – there are kids with dreadlocks, and broken packs, and burnt skin, but Dilly Hearne is not among them. It is late afternoon at the Algeciras terminal. With a shudder Maurice Hearne reaches sharply for his upper back and shows a glance of fear –

Did you ever get a whistling-type pain out the left lung, Mr Redmond?

Is it one of those sinister-type pains that you've never had before, Mr Hearne?

'Tis, yeah.

Give it time, it'll be like an old pal to you.

Maurice leans in to his friend, and he speaks with fear and very quietly now.

I'm fifty-one years to fucken Jesus, Charlie.

You rang the bell, Maurice. Whatever happens. You got more out of it than I did.

That's true.

I'm a tragic case.

Ah here.

Charlie Redmond? I'd bring a tear to a glass eye. I mean I stood up in front of my mother a bright-eyed little boy. Angelic? You could have stuck me on a holy picture. The mother thought she had the Lamb of God on her hands. And did you know that I was a stepdancer, Maurice? As a young child?

That I did not know.

I took medals for it. I could have pinned 'em across my chest, one side to the other, and halfway around my back. Tears of pride running down the mother's little jaws. The woman nearly passing out from the pride. Until she tipped backwards off a balcony in Rosscarbery after three quarters of a bottle of Cork dry gin. Which was another mark left on me. But my big problem was energy.

Who're you fucken telling?

I was a case of too much energy. It had to find its outlets. And you know where it found them.

Energy is tricky, Charlie. For the males. You know I even gave up on the self-abuse? On account of energy concerns.

As well off. You had the shoulder hanging out of its socket, Moss.

I went cold turkey. I put it in a jar altogether. Thinking it would restore the essence in some way.

How'd you get on?

Poisoned myself. I was going around the place with the eyes on extensions. There wasn't a woman aged seventeen to seventy wasn't taking the lairy glance. I was drooling like a dog, Charlie.

Self-abuse can't be left aside lightly, Maurice. It can be a necessary release for a gent at any age.

Strange the way it don't get mentioned in adult life. And we're all at it.

Hammer and tongs. But why's it strange we keep quiet? What are you after? Analysis of technique?

I'm fairly set in my ways at this stage, Charlie. Being honest.

So you're back at it?

Oh, God, I am, yeah.

Mother Fist and her five daughters.

That never once let me down.

*

The darkness again is falling – it drags its covers across the Straits in a slow, moving tide. There will be boats on the water tonight, but not for a while.

At the café bar, in the terminal, the fans whine and the note has a glassiness or brittle taint, and there is a low babble of Spanish and Moroccan voices for an undertow.

Maurice and Charlie take to the high stools at the bar and decide, in silent consultation, on an order of brandies.

What's it in the Spanish, Charlie? The brandy?

Hennessy, Charlie says.

It might put a tune back into us?

Might well do, Maurice.

He calls for two of the Hennessy. As they are poured, the moment seems to flicker and glow, and the past becomes unstable. It shifts and rearranges back there.

As he slowly turns on his barstool, Maurice Hearne is dialled back to a time almost two decades past, a time in his life of unnatural disturbances, a time that almost brought his girl to her end.

Chapter Six

AN ENCHANTMENT

Around Berehaven, and in Seville, and in Málaga,
and around Berehaven again, in December 1999

This is from her shadow time. She was four years old. It was
the end of the century and it felt like such a strange time.
It felt like everybody was saying goodbye. The early winter
was cold and clear. They were living outside Berehaven. It
was raw up on the hill. He was in a serious condition. He
was all stirred up and clairvoyant somehow, and he wanted
to fuck all around him.

*

He was in the spare room mostly. They were having a bad
spell. In the mornings he would look in on Cynthia,
sleeping. The way that her lips moved. Her dreams, they
must have been livid. He'd look in on Dilly, as she halfways
slept, and when she turned he spoke to her, and it was crazy
stuff – he told her there were tiny elves in her hair. On
each strand of her hair they rested and were weightless

there. He said they'll protect you if anything bad should happen to me.

He was certain the bad times were coming.

*

They had named the terrace of nine houses Ard na Croí. It hovered above the town, the cold harbour. They could not sell the houses – the streak of bad luck continued. The terrace was deserted but for the three of them. They were in the last house along – number nine – and in the morning he'd sit and drink coffee out of the Tangier pot and look out to the old mound and it was breathing. He was sure of it. It was a vivid winter and bright, and it was treeless up there, and the birds showed even in the hard season against the bareness and the rocks, a string of bright finches across the grey in a flit like jewels of red and gold, and it was beautiful, and he could take it no more. He'd make words on his lips and not know where they came from. He started to see the sky as a kind of membrane. His head felt like it was the size of the planet. The sky was just a casing for his pulsing brain and it was too thin. He might explode like a star.

*

He had been unsettled for months, for the winter long. There were hysterical sunsets. There were jealous rages. In the morning, when the sun came through, there was brief mercy in its light, and he might for a half-hour be passable. In the night, when the sea moaned, it was an insinuation, and he was certain she was fucking around on him. He went along with every mad vision his diseased mind could offer. He could watch every scene as it played. Every man she spoke to was involved in it. He started to keep a fix on the hours of her day. He went out and then doubled back to try and surprise her. He parked on the high road and watched the house in the dark. The engine idling, and his poor heart racing. He hadn't slept right since they'd moved into the place. In the night he'd lie there and listen to the wind speak, the rain. And how the sea moaned.

*

The sunsets were biblical. If they were having a civil day, they'd drive out the road in the evening towards the end of the peninsula and watch the sky fill up with the blood of heaven and say goodbye to the day, and Dilly would flap her little paw at the falling sun and she'd say

bye now, so long, good luck

in the strange old woman's voice she had lately been affecting, as the sun went down behind the dark sea, and these drives were an immense relief, actually, because here we are all safe and counted in the pod of the car – one, two, three – safe and fucking counted.

*

The winter days were bright and slow. They were off most of the drugs. The hours were heavy and cumbersome and moved by like old horses. He fucked a crusty girl in Bantry, thinking it would take the rage out of him; the rage intensified. When he phoned his mother in the evenings, she'd ask how things were going, and there was motherly insinuation to the question. Are you not so great in yourself, Moss? He said that it was difficult to say.

*

In the car one Sunday morning he performed a sex act on a bar girl he knew from Berehaven and thought it might wipe the brain for him. It did not wipe no fucking brain. Instead a curious image came to him.

*

It was the image of Gulliver pinned to the earth, the skin stretched out in a thousand sharp pulls and tacked, his wife, his child, his mother, his dead father, the green corridor, his crimes and addictions, his enemies and worse, his friends, his debtors, his sleepless nights, his violence, his jealousy, his hatred, his insane fucking lust, his wants, his eight empty houses, his victims, his unnameable fears and the hammering of his heart in the dark and all the danger that moved through the night and all of his ghosts and all that his ghosts demanded from him and the places that he had been to in his life and longed for again, and the great pools of silence in the bone hills above – what lives inside those fucken hills? – and the solitude that he so badly craved, and the peace he so needed, and the love he needed, and he was just a young man still, in essentials, he was really very young – but, yes, he was pinned to the fucken earth all right.

And oh God how much he wanted to go.

*

The boats put out to sea. The trawlers moved their rust in the winter sun. The harbour was a skivvy to itself always. He was in a strange, hybrid state. He thought about driving his car into the ocean.

At night, beside her, if he was allowed entry to the bed, there in the sodium gloom of the terrace lights through the window, his fingertips trailed lightly the mark of her tattooed tit – the number 13. He wished to cause her pain. He wished to devote the last of his life to her. They had opened old ground they should have left sleeping.

He looked in on Dilly, as she dreamed and soaked up the early-morning dark, and he thought about a goodbye – a goodbye to his child – and how the fuck that might be.

*

His jealousy that winter was a green fever but sometimes it lifted and he could live his own life, even if only for a few hours, breathing from the loins, it seemed, aimed into his life at a projection directly from the loins, and designed to a single purpose only. He knew women in Berehaven and in Bantry. He brought them gifts of cocaine and black cannabis oil. He spoke to them quietly and did not tell any jokes and he could read their sex thoughts before they came to their lips. It was the season of hopeless lust. The seed was telling itself to spread out, to disseminate, and quickly. Also, the seed was telling the news that death would come, and it might even come soon.

*

Of course he wanted to be caught at his games and burned alive for them and his ashes scattered to the four winds, the sea.

Also, if she was fucking somebody else, he had better fuck anyone within his reach, had better fuck anything that was up from its fours, fuck anything with lungs, cognition, opposable thumbs.

This was the logic that was in place.

*

But still there would come a night with Cynthia of reprieve, when they were themselves again, when they were back in their own flesh again, when they could sit silently and alone with each other for three noble hours and stare into the flames. And then calmly and meanly fuck each other on the rug thrown down on the floor.

And the winter, it was cold and clear.

If you could only sleep, she said, it might lift from you.

The century blew out the shapes of its last short beautiful days.

And in a deep tristesse they sat on the rug on the floor, and outside in the night the black mound sent up its sighs, and they talked for a while about the money that was left and all the money that was gone from them and it was a strange comfort.

But on the breeze of the tristesse a sour shudder came through the room and she turned to him, as they drank white rioja that had warmed in the glass, and she said that actually she could smell it off him.

I can smell it off your fucking face, she said.

*

I mean what kind of a cunt do you take me for, Maurice? What kind of a fucking halfwit that you think I can't smell it off you? I'm not supposed to smell it when you bring it home to me? After whatever fucking skank you've been with? So who was it today? Who've you been fucking today? Tell me it's not the little cod-eyed cunt below in the Haven Bar?

Ah, Cynthia, he said, listen to me.

With her skinny fucking arse! And you know what's going to happen? You're going to bring eleven types of fucking disease into this house! Because everything off a fucking boat she's been hung off! It'll drop the fuck off you, Maurice! And you might be as well off! But then you come in here? With your doey fucking eyes! You come in here? With your where've-you-been, Cynthia? Because your diseased fucking brain, it can't bear to think you're with someone that somebody else might want to fuck and you ate my fucking life! You ate it! I was left to fucking lie there and not know if you were dead or alive! In fucking Tangier! In fucking Málaga! I was fucking left, Maurice!

*

He stayed until he could bear it no more, and then he stayed for a while longer, and then he went. It was in the middle of the night. He left on the beat of a cold-hearted moment and did so without thinking about it, really. He just got in the car and drove until he was out of road and then he climbed into the sky. He had not said goodbye.

*

When he rose up to himself again, alone, it was in the white city of Seville.

It was night in winter.

He sat for a while at the base of a monument in the plaza. The image in stone of some old slaughter hound above him. A troupe of Japanese kids milled and smiled. A busker wailed a ballad of gloomy, gypsy love. Maurice clicked his fingers not in time with the song but that he might convince himself of life.

He walked the plaza and passed a payphone and then another. If he called and heard her voice, or if he heard his daughter's voice, he would have no choice but to go back, and he could not go back.

He went to his pension. The interior patio was whispery with ferns. He lay shivering in a room set off from it. It was cold as the moon. It was so cold he could feel his blood move. He must have looked close to death passing through, because the pension owner, unbidden, knocked at the door and gave him a single fat orange and four paracetamol. She said she hoped he'd feel better soon. It was the most perfect orange he had ever seen. It glowed like new love. He was in so much pain he could barely drink.

These were blue nights in Spain. He finished the bottle
that was before him. He lay beneath the thin covers of a
bone-hard single bed. There was a guidebook on the
bedside locker and he read for a while to distract himself
and huddled in misery he turned with brittle fingers
the pages and read that in the year 1031 a man called
Abu al-Qasim declared that Seville was independent
from the Caliphate of Córdoba, and it was thus that he
became the King of Seville and was titled Abbad the
First.

The words caught and moved again on Maurice's lips as he
lay in the freezing room –

the King-of-Seville, the King-of-Seville

– and even when he put the book down and turned the
light off the words continued to roll –

the King-of-Seville, the King-of-Seville

– and fell into a kind of rhythm, actually –

the King-of-Seville, the King-of-Seville

– a rhythm that was somehow languorous and calming. His
new reality might yet hold.

*

Could he remove all the hooks of sentiment from himself?
The hooks that grapple on the softest parts. A small wood-
land creature turned over to reveal its soft white belly – this
was Maurice Hearne in the winter's night. Must turn this
fucking brain off –

– must turn this brain off and try to forget that I have
burned my family down.

*

All drugs are sexed. Cocaine is male. Heroin is a girl. They
had lain together with the girl. Alone in the cold pension he
thought of Cynthia quietly and of their time together. He
rehearsed all their old times. When they lived first in the flat
at St Luke's Cross – before Dilly even – the flat that looked
down on Summerhill, over Kent Station and the sidings,
across the river and the docks beyond. They sat on the couch
by night and smoked dope and sometimes a little heroin as
they looked out over the lights and bowl of the city and
listened to their records. The vinegary note as the heroin
burned over foil was the smell that went beyond sex. He spat
the stone of a green olive at her bare thigh. She held things
unsaid within – sly deposits – and it was her secrecies that
enslaved him. They shared a telepathy. They spoke darkly to
each other in bed. They threatened violence against each
other and bit. They were most of the days and nights
together. As they watched from their eyrie at St Luke's, the
winter crept in to smother the city with greys and dense
mists and the city fell to a drugged slumber. It was moving to
watch its lights burn through the riversmoke at dusk.

*

It was too cold to just lie there. He got up and went out to
the night and the streets. He walked the turns of the Jewish
town under a scimitar moon and found the one bar that
was always left open for the night. He sat at the tile

counter and ordered a white rum. The barman served him
as though from a bad dream disturbed. There was a gaggle
of early-morning workers girding themselves for the day
ahead – a few cops, it looked like, and a set of stout, short-
legged postmen drinking coffee with condensed milk and
brandy. Maurice beaked at his rum and it brought up the
acid taste of betrayal. But he had to keep his hand moving
across the pages of the night.

There was a payphone mounted on the counter. He knew
the number by heart and knew that at half past five in the
morning she would answer because in the hills above
Málaga his Karima kept foxy hours. She laughed at once at
the torture in his voice.

Oh, Maurice, she said, what have you done now, have you
killed somebody?

She said he must send them a letter. Don't call, write. He
ordered another rum. His life was being arranged somewhere
beyond himself. Just over there.

*

Cynthia, he wrote, I'm sorry that it's come to this. I don't
feel I can be healthy for you now or for Dilly. I'm not right
in myself. I'd only poison the house. But I'm doing okay
here and I'm safe. I'll be in touch soon. Nothing's
happened. It's just all these things have got me down. I
need to be on my own for a while. I want to kiss you both
very much. But I'm very ashamed. I've done a lot that's
wrong.

*

It was one of those old Andalusian bars that had not closed in years. In the small hours it made a dismal music. The barman drooped a heavy eye over the football pages. He had the look of a long shift off him. A truck went over the cobblestones, grumbling. What does a child of four know? How soon might she forget him?

Karima said that he should come to stay with her and he could rest and be well. The ridiculous facts of his life paraded past on the tile counter of the bar, grinning like minstrels and taunting. He was from a line of madmen centuries deep. Who have all these years crawled beneath the skin of the night and trembled there. Who were found shaking in the corners of wet Irish fields. Who were found crawling the rocks and in the seacaves. Found on hospital wards, and in bars, and in the depths of the woods.

The morning at its slow length came.

*

A week passed. He went to walk for a while in the hills above Málaga. A jet from the army base screamed to open the sky. A dead hotel was chained up, its windows blind. A dog carcass rotted down to salty bones. Far beneath, the blue sea trembled and broke up. As he walked his lips made words – he spoke again to Dilly and Cynthia quite madly, beseechingly.

The gist of it: would ye not be as well off without me?

Karima waited at the bottom of the road in her tiny blue Japanese car. She drove fucking hairdryers always. She

smiled at him: her broken mouth, her beautiful eyes.
Shoot me up between the toes and tell me that you love
me.

They went instead to a bar in a mountain village. They
picked at a ración of tortilla and drank cortados and
Jameson whiskey. A television played high and silently in
the corner. The barman switched channels for a mystic
show. The mystic lady stared into the camera blackly. Here
we go again, Maurice Hearne thought. It was a provincial
show, low budget – somebody who looked like she might be
the mystic's sister passed in behind her with Lidl bags as the
prophecy was made. A phone number for private consulta-
tions appeared beneath the mystic. Maurice took a pen from
the corner and made a note of it. Karima laughed. The
barman turned up the sound.

*

He called the mystic's line that night. He said that he did
not have the language but he was told that was no problem.
He entered the details of his card. He was put through to
her. In slow, careful English she said that she could hear the
trouble in his voice. It was of a yellow colour. It was
anxiety. He told her that yes, he was in a bad way. No
kidding, she said. He told her that he had done a terrible
thing and the worst of it was that maybe it was the right
thing. He said that he felt turned in a certain direction by a
power that was beyond himself. He said the feeling of this
was not always terrible. She said that it might be God, or it
might be his enemy, or perhaps it was encantamiento – she
did not have the word in English but he could guess at it,
enchantment. She said that it could be a white or a black

107

enchantment. It might forever be impossible to say. She asked him to be silent for a few moments and only to sound his breath to the phone and try to slow it. In this way he sounded out the hollows of himself. After a few moments had passed, the mystic said –

What's the first word that comes to your mind?

Ummera, he said.

*

Karima lived among a splay of cluster pines in the mountains that looked down to the city, the sea. There was a weird owl above them articulating by night mournfully in the pines. The lights of the city burned coldly down there. Karima lay her skinny bones in the tub and Maurice shot her up between the toes. His palm rested on her thin brown calf as it flexed, as she travelled, her brown eyes closing, her broken mouth softening.

I love you, he said.

Oh fuck off, she said.

He stroked her calf and she slid an eye halfways open and made a wry and dismissive sound and she had almost the strength to laugh his hand away. They could talk to each other without speaking.

What the fuck am I made of, Karima?

The same, she implied, as each or any of us is made of, of all the words we have whispered in the night, and all the promises betrayed.

Again an army jet broke the sky.

The cluster pines bunched, trembled, shook out; the owl in outrage hooted still louder.

Beneath, the lights of the city swam briskly.

It was a week to Christmas. He helped Karima to dry off and they lay down together on the couch by the low window that looked down to the city, and after a while she could talk again. She said to forget about boats of dope. Not for long now would the money be in boats of dope.

*

When I put my hand here, he said, you have a slight . . . I'd call it a startle in the eye. A little . . . surprise?

There is no surprise, she said. I've been touched there since I was nine years old.

Ah Jesus, Karima. Send me over to the fucken dark side, why don't you?

Not dark, she said. This is life.

She lit a cigarette. She blew the smoke into his face. She tipped the rim of her glass off his and they drank a white spirit.

What does it make you think of? he said. When I touch you there?

Candy, she said.

You know how to destroy me, he said. Always. You remember when we met first? I was such a kid.

You're still a kid.

Can I give you head, Karima?

I won't feel anything.

Neither here nor there. Also what's known as a gauntlet.

What's gauntlet?

It's what you've just laid down to me.

We could live in Cádiz for a while, she said.

Why Cádiz?

I stay here, I get shot or worse, she said.

And the weird owl again made its haggard call.

*

When he woke it was still dark and the wind was low in the cluster pines. He had a bad headache. He drank half a glass of beer with some pills. He looked in on Karima, and she lay face up in the bed and she was very sick in her sleep. He went to her without making a sound and leaned down and put his lips to her forehead and said goodbye and maybe he would be back soon.

Then he stole her car and drove five miles down the mountain to the city in the dark, as he couldn't figure out the fucking lights, and at the first break of the chill winter sun he sat on the beach at Malagueta and he knew that his enchantment was a black one.

Bad luck, bad luck.

*

He flew back to Cork. He rented a car. He drove out the Macroom road. It was the shortest day of the last year. Everything craved a grand ending. Everything wanted the fade-out. As he came before the Ummera Wood, the sky was filling with the first of night and the trees were banked up densely against the sky to make a dark edifice.

The world was at its cusp and turned to begin the long, slow slide into new light, new time, and he couldn't fucking bear it.

He parked the car and got out and felt the evil of the cold damp air. He listened to the ghosts of the wood. He arranged his face for Irish weather. This was not to be under-estimated. He scrunched his eyes against the wind. He twisted his mouth against the rain. Take these gestures and repeat them, times ten thousand for the life, and times the generations, and times the epochs and the eras, and see how the effect digs beneath the skin, enters the racial soul, prepares its affront to the world, and offers it –

the King-of-Seville, the King-of-Seville

– he made the words on his lips to seek calm, but the refrain was lost to the whipping wind, the assaults of rain.

He walked into the thick dark of the Ummera Wood and

into the old growth as the longest night descended like a great sombre bird roosting.

He came to what felt like a radial point and sat on the cold wet ground, and he asked his dead for forgiveness and for permission that he might join them.

*

But he was turned by a force outside of himself. Steered on a drag of the starlight, he went back to the car and drove the narrow roads west through the sleeping county to Beara.

He drank Powers whiskey from a naggin clamped between his thighs and slowed for the bends that he knew by touch.

When he dragged through the town of Berehaven like something the devil had brought in, it was past five in the morning.

He sat by the harbour's cold lights for a while and finished the whiskey and let the seat back and tried to sleep the need away, but he could not – he had unravelled.

He drove towards Ard na Croí. He parked on the road above it. He walked along the crescent swathe of the terrace and watched the old mound breathing.

He let himself in without so much as a key scratch. He climbed the stair. He listened for their breathing. On the upstairs landing he let his breath slow until the air settled around him. His eyes came down to the gloom. He did not blurt a single movement.

He looked in on Cynthia and saw that she was not alone – the long, needle-thin figure of Charlie Redmond was beside her.

Is this going on again, he said, but quietly, and they did not wake.

He found Dilly in a hot bundle, sleeping. He leaned in and whispered to her. She moved in her sleep and spoke. He lifted her from the bed and carried her down the stairs still sleeping and out of the house – they left as quietly as he'd entered and with her arms around him, waking, she nested against the cold on his shoulder.

Dilly, he said.

*

He drove the child through the sleeping town. The movement of the car quickly closed her eyes again. He drove out to Cametringane and stopped by the slipway to the water. She rolled up from her sleep and shivered and said Daddy? Where are we, Dad? Where are we going?

We'll go home, Dill.

The long night lowered itself along the last notches of its spine – the lizard night – and if I start the car and if I just let it roll, then all of this is quickly over.

Will we, Dill?

What, Dad?

He sat in the car by the slipway and felt the tightness of

the handbrake, its tension grip, and he flicked the key to lock all the doors.

You know that I love you, Dilly?

Can we go home? she said. I'm cold.

And as she started to cry he ascended from himself – it was a shooting motion, sudden and violent, as though on a hoist – and he saw himself parked there, with the child, on the verge of their ending, not far from the town of Berehaven, on a morning in the dead of winter, and he saw the enchantment as a black aura around him.

But he breathed deeply, and then he did so once more, and he felt the life pass through himself –

let it out and let it in.

She reached to hold his hand and her touch was clammy. He licked the tears from her face like a dog. Now a new light entered the pod of the car –

From beyond the long shadow of Bere Island, the rim of the sun at last came up and Dilly's face was lit by the weak sun and she greeted the sun in her strange, olden voice –

Oh hi, hello, howya, she said.

Chapter Seven

THEIR AFFLICTIONS

At the port of Algeciras, in October 2018

Maurice Hearne sits alone in the café bar at the ferry terminal. He turns the remains of a third brandy in its glass. You keep going any way you can. The motions of the alcohol are familiar: the easy warming, the calm sustain, and now the slow grading into remorse. A melancholy hour falleth. As afflicts a gentleman of colourful history. But, if he has nothing else to his name, he has his regrets, and these are not without value to the martyr's self-portrait displayed in his mind's eye. I am fifty-one years old, he thinks, and still at least halfways in love with meself. All told you'd have to call it a fucken achievement.

He turns a swivel on the barstool, curiously. He lets the good eye roam – he checks the place out. Spain again – its old, tatty charisma. You wake up again and it's Spain again. There is another gap between boats. There may be disruptions once more on the Tangier side. Charlie

Redmond is having a mad half-hour and is doing the stations of the cross around the terminal – male energy, the excess of. Maurice feels somehow that Dilly is nearby; he knows in his blood that she is near; there is a stirring inside.

And now from the vantage of his years a terrible swoon comes down on him; Cynthia, for a moment, descends all the way through him. This is not a rare occurrence. He will never lose the feeling of the love that they had together, or the nausea of its absence.

Hate is not the answer to love; death is its answer.

*

Night and day an amusement to himself – and he'd want to be, the way the nerves are set – Charlie Redmond approaches at a relaxed, limping pace the hatch that's marked INFORMACIÓN. He leans on its tilted ledge. With a comedian's poise he waits on the timing's beat. As it falls, he addresses, with courtesy, the informaciónista – it's the same lad, with the bitter face on.

How're you getting on inside? Charlie says.

He receives no reply.

Good man yourself, he says. You've a lovely little face and you're a great worker. Anyhow. While I have you. I'm looking for three pieces of . . . información. Numero uno. Does this man here, Charlie Redmond, of Farranree, Cork city, in the Free State of Ireland, does he have a sad kind of a look to him?

He pauses with great interest, inclines his head, as if listening to the informaciónista's response, which is not forthcoming.

I hear you, boy, he says.

He turns to the terminal at large and addresses it, with his arms wide, his palms turned up.

He reckon so. Me soul is in me boots. By this fella's account? Charles Redmond? A blue-hearted old cove. And is it any wonder? After what these poor eyes have seen? The night I opened a throat up in Dillons Cross? The lad was trying to eat a chicken supper at the time. Mushy peas bouncin' off the wall. But that's all in the dim and distant. I've more to be dealing with now. Of course my arse isn't right since Málaga. Since the night of the recent unpleasantness in Málaga. The octopus looking up at me out of the plate? And the octopus wasn't the worst of Málaga. Not by any means. We needed a steer. We fucken got it too. Anyhow. While I have you?

He turns again to the hatch, leans on it, offers the homicidal grin. His volume control is shot –

Información! Numero dos! This man here, Charlie Redmond, of Farranree, in Cork city, do you reckon he has a vicious kind of a look to him?

He listens, carefully, his face warm and open before the hatch, as if the informaciónista is again giving a detailed response, which he is not. At length, Charlie shakes his head and he turns to the terminal again.

Total savage altogether, he says. By this man's account. And no wonder, some of the lanes that I've been down? Oh, quare lanes, quare lanes. I tell you this. You would not want to see Charles Redmond coming, at a peculiar hour of the night, up the northside estates, in Cork city, and the black eyes on him. I'm talking about back in the day. I mean I'm a pussy cat now. I'm weak as a kitten, in fact, but back in the day? Charlie at the door and the dog beside him? Uh-oh. Especially if there was money owed. You want to talk to the fucken dog about it? And listen. I mean dogs? I had some mighty dogs in my day. There was one fella, Shortie, an outstanding hound, he used to lick the Rizlas for me and I building a number and he could smell a squad car from three quarters of a mile off. Approx. He'd do a special little howl for it.

The ferry terminal at the port of Algeciras is by no means put out by the spectacle of Charlie Redmond addressing its haunted air – we take this very much in our stride.

I mean ye're looking at a man here, his most auspicious relationships in life have, in many ways, been with dogs. Oftentime.

He returns his attention to the hatch.

And finally, he says. Numero tres. It's the one we've all been waiting for. Three Qs is all you get and I'm not going to argue with that. You can't beat the machine. So, finally . . . Does this man here, Charlie Redmond, of Cork city, Ireland, on the evidence of what you can see right now, just here, before thee, through your busy little masturbator's eyes, does this poor Charlie have the look of a man who's known love in his life?

He listens carefully to the response that is not given.

Okay, he says, and he returns to sit on the bench.

You have me, he says. You can see it all too clearly. The nature of Charlie Red's affliction . . . I knew love but I lost it.

*

There is a ripple of energy through the building and it's anticipatory – it feels as if a boat may be about to come or go. Maurice Hearne lugs his unease from the bar downstairs to the waiting area. There comes a time when you just have to live among your ghosts. You keep the conversation going. Elsewise the broad field of the future opens out as nothing but a vast emptiness.

Think about the fucken good times, Moss, he tells himself.

The first six months on heroin with Cynthia were the most beautiful days of all time. Love and opiates – this is unimprovable in the human sphere. Like young gods they walked out. Some night coming down Wellington Road from St Luke's. Some Friday night in the rain. That was the best night that ever was.

It was kind of wild, Cynthia, wasn't it? It was all a bit too fucken wild, really.

He goes to the bench just west of the hatch marked INFORMACIÓN and joins Charlie Redmond there. His oldest friend; his old rival.

*

What's it they got now, Maurice? The word?

For which is this, Charlie?

The hydro-what's-it, Moss?

Ponic, Charlie. You mean the hydroponic?

Hydro-cuntology is what it is, Maurice. You know what it means? It means the end for the likes of you and me.

Ah, listen. We're the Antiques Roadshow. The little fuckers growing it in their own bedrooms? Under lights? The dope they're growing in the West of Ireland now you wouldn't get it in the Rif Mountains.

Or they're buying it off the fucken internet.

It's very sad to see, Charles.

It's not right, Maurice.

It's an end to a whole way of being.

The likes of you and me won't pass this way again, Moss.

They turn to look at each other, softly – the air is weighted, memorial.

We been through a lot, old pal.

Where would we even begin, Charlie?

Nights in Berehaven we kicked each other around the road?

Nights on the high seas?

The night at the Judas Iscariot?

Ah, don't go there, Charlie . . . Please.

We had our good times too, Moss.

We did, yeah.

There were times the luck turned right. Hardly the arse of a trouser between us and we'd find ourselves in Casablanca. We'd find ourselves in Puerto Banús. We'd be atein' rings around us in Marbella. There was a time the business was booming.

You know why, Charlie? Because if Irish people are martyrs for the drink, they're worse again for the dope, once they get the taste for it, because it eases the anxiety, and we're a very anxious people.

Why wouldn't we be, Moss? I mean Jesus Christ in the garden, after all that we been through? Dragging ourselves around that wet tormented rock on the edge of the black Atlantic for the months and years never-ending and the long gawpy faces screamin' for the light and the jaws operatin' on wires and the pale little yellow arses hanging out the back end of us?

Dope be the only thing get us through, Charles.

*

A ferry boat arrives from the port of Tangier. Its tired crowd straggles through the terminal. It's as if an ordeal has been passed through. The short crossing to Algeciras can play an odd music inside – trouble has passed this way before, and the old journeys reverberate still.

The men watch on as a new crowd starts to congregate – the ferry may sail again later.

Dilly Hearne enters the terminal and now she is among the crowd.

Her hair is worn in a bleached pixie crop shorn high and tightly at the sides. She wears vintage Polaroid sunglasses, a pair of men's pinstripe trousers buckled high at the waist and a white zip-up Veja hoodie. She pulls a trolley case behind her. She moves inside an aura of calm – at twenty-three years old she is already queenly.

She sees the two men on the bench by the INFORMACIÓN hatch, the way that they scan the crowd, and at once she averts her face from them, and veers away.

She goes to the bar upstairs. She watches from there and she allows her breath to slow, or she tries to. Her heart slaloms and thumps in its cage. Her blood races. She watches over the top of her sunglasses –

Yes, it's Maurice, turning his good eye around the floor, and yes, it's Charlie, rising now, heartbreakingly, and limping slowly towards the hatch on his old drag-along step.

Okay, Dilly says, and she turns to the bar and orders a brandy.

Chapter Eight

THE JUDAS ISCARIOT
ALL-NIGHT DRINKING
CLUB

In the city of Cork, in January 2000

It was a little after 4 a.m. on a January night. It was in the long, cold sleep of the winter. The shapes of the city were blocked out above the dark river, against the moonless sky. On the southside quays only the ghosts of the place traipsed by the doorways or idled on the steps of the river wall with their stories of old love. The black surface of the river moved the lights of the city about. It was hard not to believe sometimes that we were just the reflection, and that the true life existed down there in the dark water.

At the Judas Iscariot, an illicit drinking den set back a little from the quays, it was an arranged knock, a coded knock, that allowed entry and you played out the knock in a few quick hard raps, with this rhythm, like so –

*

The captain of the ship stood behind the bar counter. He surveyed the place with tranquil smile. This was Nelson Lavin, of the gold tooth and the whispery vowels. There beneath the optics he swung out a slow, benevolent scan of the room –

The Judas drew a low crowd but not an unglamorous one. Night people. Scavengers. A criminal ascendency. They were arranged at low tables in the dim light. There was an aura of trinket menace from their neck chains in the light. Over the course of a long night maybe a couple of dozen hardened souls would move in uncertain fraternity around the pools of table light.

The inclination at the Iscariot was to drink steadily but decorously. Nelson Lavin kept a watchful eye that such decorum be maintained. He loosened the brass ring on his pinkie and circled it slowly and, that the night might hold on a mellow note, he rubbed a charm on the ring with holy fingers. But his gums were swollen, and this was usually a sign for Nelson that trouble was coming.

He looked slowly around the room and reckoned the names and familiars of the place, their situations. He brought a shine the length of the counter with his bar cloth. He leaned into sleepy Vincent Keogh, the house-breaker, who was swaying somewhat on a corner stool.

Way is things shaping for you, Vincent? Bigger-picture wise?

Skaw-ways and unpleasantly, Nelson.

Throw back the shoulders for me there, Vince, and look straight out ahead of you.

He scanned the bar again, smiling –

The faces don't be right around here. This was Nelson's belief. A townful of hawky-looking dudes with sinister chins and dumpling noses.

Steve Bromell, the cocaine pedlar, was staring in fear to the low tin ceiling, as though it might cave in, but Stevie looked scared at the best of times, as often with good cause. He'd nearly miss the paranoia if ever it eased off.

Two ladies-of-love; a ponce; a prince amongst bouncers.

Discreet people.

Charlie Redmond was drinking alone but for his demons at a crowded table down the back.

There was something to be understood in the Redmond glaze, Nelson believed, in the slow, dull gaze, and the way that he was with careful deliberation ripping up the beermats.

Hard faces; burnt eyes; shebeen hours.

The vodka that turned in Charlie Redmond's long fingers made a slow, ominous swirl – the turning glass caught the low, amber lights of the Iscariot.

Nelson dipped beneath the bar hatch and crossed the room with a half-litre of Grey Goose – he laid his hand to the back of Charlie's to still the glass, and he topped it.

You know they say that vodka is uncouth, Charlie?

I was dragged up, Charlie Redmond said. Side of the road job.

The glint of humour was a reassurance, but Nelson still had the swollen feeling about his gums.

Jimmy Earls, a brothel-keeper, sat heavily over a half of Beamish stout and sipped from it and followed it with a dewdrop of Powers whiskey. He moved his lips daintily as he recounted beneath his breath the litany of his bitternesses. Rita Kane, a lady of schemes, played out for the benefit of her friend Sylvia's ears the details of an acrimonious split with Edmond Leary, a common thief, and Sylvia's left hand reached for her throat and clutched it softly, an expression of distilled Corkonian dismay. Alvin Hay, once a boxer, in the far corner wept tearlessly, with the catch of his throat opening – this was the season his wife was dying.

Out front, a sequence of knocks came in the precise arrangement – the boy fetched open the door and heads turned slowly in the room to mark the arrival of Maurice Hearne.

A face to match the night on him as he entered, but he softened it and made smiling across the room to Charlie Redmond. Charlie stood to greet him, and the men embraced.

Trouble out west, trouble in Berehaven, was the word on the wind that Nelson Lavin had caught. Love trouble – the worst strain. He attended carefully with his cloth to the run and turn of the grain of his counter's wood.

The room kept its breath. It held on a moment of violent possibility. Maurice sat in the chair opposite Charlie's. He kicked the legs out in front of himself. Charlie rested his long, thin face on the knit of his hands beneath the chin. When he began to speak, there was a hungry pleading in his eyes.

Nelson considered the room's resources should unpleasantness occur. Jimmy Earls was put together like a Victorian bridge but not a man of stout convictions since a brush with death the night a knife was bared in Cobh, a kidney scarred the result of it. Alvin might be useful, if the mood took him. The boy who worked the door was of an intemperately brave stock and could be a help. There was no knowing how the night could spin out. Discreetly, Nelson felt under the counter for the reassurance of his whitethorn cosh.

Outside, the wind was getting higher – this was at every fucking chance it got an operatic place.

The wind blew the lights of the city about.

The lights moved back and forth in a slow, narcotic swaying on the black skin of the river.

At the Judas Iscariot the two old friends sat and consulted each other. This was trouble of a particular timbre – Nelson Lavin could read it at a half-glance.

Jimmy Earls tiptoed his great bulk barside and by a flutter of his eyelashes summoned Nelson to a huddle.

You watching over?

Am I the fuck.

There's smoke coming out the ears, Nelson.

Been trouble yonder?

In Berehaven. It's reported.

On account of the beore?

Good-looking woman. In fairness. And fierce.

These were fabled people. These were tricky times. They were in a moment of dangerous splendour. The men were lizardly, reptilian. They wore excellent fucking shoes. Nelson carefully with Jimmy Earls kept an eye on the confrontation. It was a smiling one, yet, and soft-voiced. These were deliberate people. Why should they meet just here, just now? Maybe it needed to be seen, and recounted.

Charlie Redmond leaned in to confide. He spoke seriously, and Maurice Hearne leaned in and listened. Now he reached for Charlie's glass of vodka and took a sip from it.

Covertly, with fear and anticipation mingled, Nelson Lavin and Jimmy Earls watched the show from the sidelines.

Way is they fixed generally, you reckon?

Not great, Nelson said. They lost a boat below last year.

Bother on the home front be the last thing they need.

These two went way back, Nelson knew. Barrack Street in the '80s. A pub called the Three Ones. An eyes-sideways-in-your-head job. Charlie and Moss at the back table, barely shaving. Their dope stashed behind the cross on the wall of the deadhouse across the road. Younger fellas running it for them. He served Alvin Hay a Drambuie and said, friend, catch a hold of yourself. Life or death, each day has its insistences, and there is nothing we can do to gainsay them.

You can't beat the machine, Alvie, he said.

Would he swing by the table? Try to get a sense of it? They were huddled close in and speaking with animation. Jimmy Earls stayed barside, sensing Nelson's worry – Jimmy considered himself A Rock in edgy circumstances. Also, by constitution, he was out for the full of his mouth. He was fetched up another half of Beamish – it was Jimmy Earls's life-long conviction that pint glasses were ignorant-looking. As the black stout settled, he took out his little can of 3-in-One oil from the inside pocket and added five drops – counting them off – to the glass.

Shocking habit, Nelson said, as he did every night.

It's the lubrication is the only thing keepin' the lungs straight in me back, Jimmy Earls said.

Now bravely Nelson slipped out and swung from behind his bar and roamed the shebeen floor. He took up a glass here, a glass there. He made a precise shuffle around back of the Hearne, Redmond table – they'd invaded Russia with less complication than the way some nights Nelson Lavin had to move around his own fucking bar-room. He tuned in, briefly, to their low, serious talk.

Can the liver and chips be bate for a hangover, Maurice? Charlie Redmond said.

Not if you were stuck into them above in the Uptown Grill, Charlie.

The Uptown, Charlie said. Regal premises.

Jesus Christ, Nelson thought – their devotion. As he sidled back to the other side of their table, he caught Maurice's eye and enquired by a small shaping of the lips if a drink was required.

I'm good a while, Nelson. The night's a pup yet.

The men continued to talk; Nelson returned to the bar and danced the deft and pleasing little move that took him beneath the hatch.

Well? Jimmy Earls said.

They're talking about the liver and chips above in the Uptown Grill.

None finer in the town, Jimmy Earls said, and sipped his stout, grimaced.

I think they could be working themselves up to it, Nelson said.

Outside, the last few taxis drifted as stoically as old cows. The drivers looked lonely in the warm handsome yellow of their cabs. The squad cars, with disinterest, took slow turns about the town. The guards knew well of the Judas Iscariot and silently approved – it was a system of containment.

Nelson took the cloth to the bar's counter and worked it with the turn of the knot and the run of the wood's grain.

He eyed the significant table and wondered how long before he might swing by again. Or maybe send Jimmy Earls by?

Jimmy Earls took the instruction eager as a small dog taking a stick and headed for the facilities. He went by their table unseen – even at twenty-two and a half stone he could disappear in a room the size of this, and smaller again.

As he went past, he heard –

What way did it happen, Charlie? Was there stuff that you said to her?

The moment was approaching. I could be as well staying in the jacks altogether, Jimmy thought, with the lad in me hand. The way things might be shaping out there. He stood and sighed and counted off the drops as they spattered the urinal tile. With the maggot in me hand, he thought – it's the maggots is the cause of half the consternation around this place.

Nelson beneath the counter gripped the whitethorn cosh for its heft. There had been blood on the premises too recently, necessitating a conversation with the superintendent at the Bridewell Station and a month's closure – Nelson Lavin had been a month at home on his ownsome watching Judge Judy at five in the morning. Jimmy Earls reappeared, noiselessly, in that shattering way of his. His hoarse, soft, whoremaster's voice came across the counter –

They're getting into it now, he said. Goodo.

The hot face on Jimmy read Showtime. Something in the air had changed. There was information in the room like a waft. It was strong as the singe of burnt hair. Vinnie Keogh glanced over his shoulder with morbid unease. Sylvia tipped the back of Rita's hand – don't look now.

But somehow all eyes were drawn to the table at precisely the moment Maurice Hearne picked up the glass of vodka and flung its contents in Charlie Redmond's face. He sat there smiling as he set the glass down again and Charlie, who had not flinched, neither did he now react. He sat there perfectly still and he did not wipe the vodka from his face. He just let it roll down his cheeks and drip onto the table, his expression impassive.

Now Maurice addressed his old friend quickly, directly, neither smiling nor unsmilingly, and Charlie's expression remained even and calm. Jimmy Earls reached for his overcoat set on the hook beneath the bar's rim but as quickly he replaced it there – this night could be legend.

Nelson worked the bar cloth along the counter's wood and grain. The gums were alive in his mouth. Over the motion of the cloth he watched as Maurice aimed more words across the table, and Charlie Redmond did not in any way respond. Was it accusation only that flew, or was there a sense of litany, an outpouring of long grievance? It was impossible to predict what turns might be taken when a woman got in the middle of things. He believed that both men had in the past killed. Jimmy Earls exhaled luxuriously to savour the trouble on the air even before it came properly to pass – I was there on the night of it.

What way you reading it, Nelson?

Jesus only knows.

You think something should be said?

You feeling valiant, Jimmy?

You could fetch 'em a drink over maybe? Innocent little face on you. Make light of it, kind of?

Maybe.

In the gesture there would be word that no harm was yet done. We can proceed gently even still. He took down the bottle of Grey Goose, picked up two fresh glasses, ducked and turned beneath his hatch. He reached back to lay the bar cloth over his forearm. That proper fucking order might be maintained. He carried his saintly face to their table – Maurice leaned back, his eyes widened; Charlie allowed half a natty smile. Nelson primly but without remark mopped the few spits of vodka from the table, placed the two fresh glasses, halfways filled them and returned to the bar.

When he was behind it again he turned to find the men raise their glasses in salute to him. The room was in the grip of all this wonderfully now. Maurice Hearne and Charlie Redmond leaned in again to talk. Jimmy Earls blinked rapidly to pass an admiring remark on Nelson's poise.

Outside, there was an eerie night music. The wind moved across the river, the wires swayed, and the lights of the city broke up on the water to mix their colours, but these reformed again sharply as the wind rested.

It was a little after five bells.

133

Now Charlie Redmond was doing all the talking. It was painful stuff, was Nelson's read, and Jimmy Earls agreed — the way that Charlie's lips moved, his sombre grey eyes.

A heart-to-heart we have on us hands, Jimmy said.

Indeed.

You know what they say about the beore?

What's that, Jimmy?

She run the show. She call the moves. She name the moment.

They always say that about the beore.

Maybe it's account of her way they says it. She be a put-manners-on-you type.

At the far table the men's voices came up. The room as one turned to the voices. They were by no means roaring but an agitation was evident, and passion. Nelson Lavin took the whitethorn in his hand. He watched the situation stony-faced, like a referee. Their voices quietening again, Maurice and Charlie leaned in. Eyes elsewhere in the room averted. Jimmy Earls leaned in —

Will I swing past again?

Do, Jimmy. Take the feel of things.

Noiselessly the fat whoremaster glided across the floor. Jimmy Earls the brothel creeper. A very tidy sort in his great bulk. Aim for the porcelain, swing by the hard table. The creased fold thick as a pound coin on the back of Maurice Hearne's neck – there was a great tension there, while a certain blithe-ness, unhelpfully, in Jimmy's opinion, had descended over Charlie Redmond's eyes. As he moved past their table, again unseen, he caught from the Redmond these words –

Because Karima's a schemin' cunt.

Jimmy Earls across no-man's-land made it again to the facil-ities. He stood once more with the lad in his hand. He looked to the small window set high – there was no way he'd wriggle through. What if a weapon was now produced? Already, even as he passed through the events of the night, Jimmy at the back of his mind was framing the narrative – he was thinking how he would tell it.

When he passed by the table again, he saw that Maurice had clamped Charlie's hand to it and he was speaking to him intensely, urgently.

Nelson had one hand under the bar – we all knew what that meant.

Well?

Who the fuck's Karima and she at home?

Who?

A Karima?

Foreign-sounding.

And a cunt apparently.

This is getting heated, Jimmy.

Hope it's not someone's old doll getting put down?

Should I put them out?

Might only push it to the edge of things.

The events quickened –

Charlie Redmond shot up from the table so quickly he sent his chair toppling backwards.

Maurice Hearne reclined, and cruelly smiled, and knit his hands behind his head.

Charlie picked up his glass of vodka and crossed the floor and stood alone at the end of the bar and there he held himself with grace. He sipped from his drink. He looked directly ahead.

Hard to gauge how long had passed – the air of the room was suspended, taut – before Maurice rose and crossed the floor, glass in hand, and he stood beside Charlie Redmond then and tipped the rim of his glass against his friend's.

Of the dozen or so unreliable narrators left in the room at this small hour, all would claim to have seen precisely what happened next – except for Nelson, who considered himself fortunate to be on the other side of the bar – and, in fact, Jimmy Earls would claim even to have *heard* what happened next, heard precisely the sound that was made when Maurice Hearne in a single movement took the knife from his pocket, dropped to a kneeling position and plunged the knife into the cup of Charlie Redmond's right knee, but it was the withdrawal of the knife that did the damage, for it was in this motion that he sliced the ligament, and it was this ripping sound that Jimmy Earls vowed he would carry with him to the deadhouse walls, and with it the single dull gasp that Charlie made.

And it was no more than that, no more than a dull gasp.

Chapter Nine

NATURAL MYSTIC

At the port of Algeciras, in October 2018

And now, by night, the port of Algeciras is humming. There is movement across the Straits. The skin of the dark water roils up and froths. It's as if there's a party going on down there. Rising on the air is a sense of witchery and fever.

In the terminal Dilly Hearne sits at the café bar. She fades deftly into the scenery. Turning an owlish half-swivel on the stool, she can see that the men are still in place downstairs. She wants to go to them quite badly. This is an astonishment to her. She wants to hear their voices. A tannoy announcement breaks out –

. . . llegará otro servicio desde Tánger y podrá ir otro servicio . . .

Another boat will come, and a boat may go. She has the language easily now, but she hears it better than she speaks it. She swivels back to the bar again. She has been a little more than three years in Spain. It feels like half a life has gone by since she left Ireland.

*

She walked on the first day through the streets of Málaga, and yes maybe there was a steely look, with a fixed jut to the jaw, as if seeking something mysterious, some new kind of volition, as if decided there was only one thing for it, there is only one thing that can save me now – I have got to leave this skin behind.

The day was hot; the air so dry. The city felt intense, close-in. An amputee sprawled on the corner of Calle Larios and the Alameda Principal arranged his stump beneath calm, medieval eyes and she was drawn to him oddly.

She crouched by the wreckage of the man and rested her backpack for a while, and she asked if he had seen the travellers – the Inglese, the Irlandese?

He said, Do you mean those kids with the dreadlocks in their hair? Those kids who go about with the dogs?

She said, Yeah, those are the ones.

She wanted to go to Maroc and live in one of the camps. She wanted a place that did not know the meaning of her grief. She wanted to travel to the far recesses of herself and see what she might find back there.

*

She watches without fear as Maurice and Charlie rise up from the bench. Something in the way they move has taken the fear away. They aim for the escalator and the bar again, with their blameless faces, as though on an impromptu expedition.

Dilly skulls her drink and lays down a few coins and drags her trolley across the floor of the bar – it follows her like a rolling accusation, seems to announce her presence, but she knows how to absent herself from the eyes. She keeps her head moving, her face turning. She looks everywhere but in the direction of the approaching men. The terminal throbs fiercely now. She wades into the bodies –

There's a topless old hombre in nylon trackpants drinking an amber spirit and rolling his tongue over his teeth as he watches her go by, and she burns the fucking look off his face with a single, darted stare.

There's a grinning scut in a beige corduroy suit sitting on the floor outside the bar and sucking on a tin of Cruzcampo beer and he may have just about pissed himself.

There's a blind lottery-ticket seller leaning back into his patch of wall, his palms flat on the marble, as if he's holding the place up, and the strain is telling in the awful viscous whites of his eyes.

The crowd has thickened for the last heave of the night.

The quick gabbling ham-eater mouths are silky-greasy in the hard terminal light.

There is crazy fucking denim everywhere.

Maurice and Charlie pass by obliviously within a few feet of

her. She stares at the floor and drags her trolley along as the
men go into the bar.

Jesus Christ – the age that's gone on them.

She descends by the escalator and goes and sits on their
bench near the hatch that is marked . . .

INFORMACIÓN

*

For the first months she lived in Granada in a cheap
pension there. There was an atmosphere of old mystery in
the city, a tangy resonance at sundown. The place spoke
of broken hearts. She had eight hundred euros and then it
was seven three five. She kept it under her pillow and
counted it first thing in the mornings – it was going in
one direction only. Six four zero. She was determined
never to go home again. The first of the blue Granada
morning came up. She was down to five three five. There
was a bleeding Jesus on the wall – she stared at it in
the dawn half-light – a sexy bleeding Jesus in a loincloth
on the wall. The twisted mouth, the come-hither – fuck
off.

The last thing her mother said to her was you must never
come back here, Dilly.

And in Granada, in those first months, she slept mostly by
day, and when she dreamed it was of desert places and
sometimes she woke to the cemetery hush of the afternoon
lull and she wanted to go and lie on a cold desert floor in
the evening among the flowers of the dusk – the dull

amethysts, the quiet rubies – and let her blood flow to feed them.

*

But now she wants to hear the men speak. She gets up from the bench and drifts a couple of dozen yards east. She leans against the wall and stares into her phone and pretends to scroll as they pass by on their way back from the bar.

In fact, she never goes online any more, because technology is the pigs' white evil, and online is where they find you, and it's how they keep track of you.

She has thirty-two fake Spanish passports sewn into the lining of her trolley case.

Maurice and Charlie cross the floor to the bench again.

She follows but at a measured distance.

As she goes by, three tall and skinny men from the bad end of Marrakesh look her over from their slouches against the concession wall. They speak quietly, sidemouthedly, to each other.

She passes slowly rearside of the bench just as Maurice and Charlie resume their positions, and she could almost reach out and touch the backs of their heads. She listens –

I'd get a dog again, Charlie says, but I don't know if I have the length of a small dog left in me.

You definitely don't have two dogs in you, Maurice says.

*

In Granada she moved into a cave in the Albaicín district with a few English people and their dogs. The rent was almost nothing and anyway it was never paid. The dogs were outright comedians. Mostly the cave houses were illegal; they held no permits. Her room was tiny and windowless and wistful. Like a fucking womb. Like a tomb. The walls the colour of bone and ashes, the low roof pressing down – living in the cave turned into a pressure situation. It was not easy to shed the old skin. She was very lonely there. The cave was set on the hills on the vault of the city. The sun raged. She was a lizard of the Albaicín. The English people, she wouldn't call them friends exactly, but she was among the dogs and that was something. She was a consort of the dogs – of Coco, Ellie and Bo. She let them sleep in the room with her. She whispered to them sometimes about her people. The months in this way passed by.

And in the Albaicín in the hot afternoon sun some ragged kids in a tangle played a kind of tag or chase game in the square and Dilly laid out the disks of the sun on a cloth of black velvet.

With her magnifier she had all summer made designs of spirals, fertility symbols, crosses; she had made marks of the occult and a sheela-na-gig.

She sat on the ground in the square with her back to the warm stone. She no longer felt like a beggar sitting in this way, at supplicant height. It was to do with how you displayed your face.

*

There is no word on the next ferry out. There are tannoy messages, but they contradict each other. The men remain on the bench as watchful as hawks and dumb as spoons. She wants to approach them but she cannot yet. She drifts upstairs to the café bar again. She moves in the sequence of a disturbed dream. There are voices at the edges of the dream. They come from the violent past. The dream is in the shape of the ferry terminal at the port of Algeciras.

She wants to talk to the men. In fact, she wants to be held. She could throw up at this idea. She wants to go further south in Morocco this year. She wants to go into the desert. She orders a slice of tortilla. The barman is as stoned-looking as a fucking koala. The tortilla is too dry. It tastes like a sacrifice. A jangle of bad nerves zips across the bar's air –

A stocky man at the counter clutches his groin, groans, unhandles himself, lays his forehead on the metal counter. He clutches his groin once more. Cries out.

A tiny sultana-faced man wearing lilac slacks and a blazer beneath a pompadour hair-do arrives in and tries to sell socks out of a plastic bag.

Dilly goes and looks down over the balustrade to the bench downstairs, and now in perfect tandem Maurice and Charlie look up – they have been drawn on the line of her gaze.

*

One day she went to Málaga to sell the disks of the sun. She picked a spot by the cathedral walls. Fate sent a long Maghrebi in a djellaba to appear beside her. Fastidiously he

145

unrolled a black cloth. He set down some wooden figurines of princely Africans. Dilly tried to read from her paperback – gore; American; a serial killer loose under the Ohio moon – but the words would not stick. The hours unrolled like a great river. There were no customers for herself or for the Maghrebi.

She sat with her phone and looked at tattoos on Instagram. Technology was the white evil on the air. She watched clips of laughing dogs. She stood and stretched out the kinks, and she considered the African figurines that so precisely replicated their seller. He was very tall, maybe six and a half feet tall, and he stood like Job in the afternoon heat.

Where you from? she said.

He smiled in a tired way and gestured towards the docks, the sea, somewhere that lay beyond the sea.

You know the policía here? she said. You know what they're like?

He just shrugged, lazily, who-knows-anything.

Are there other places in town? she said. Where the policía won't move us?

Maybe, he said.

She picked up one of his figurines and turned it in her hand.

The fuck where'd you get these anyhow?

A place near the airport, he said. You can get the airport bus. It goes right by the place.

He smiled and crouched and knit his thin limbs to look over the sun disks. She took out the magnifier from her pack and showed it.

With the sun, she said.

He nodded at the idea and admired the disks.

I come from a place, she said, that's a long way from the sun.

Where?

Ireland. Irlandes?

I've never been.

You're nearly as well off out of it.

Is it not nice?

Oh, it's a tremendous place but tricky, you know?

Tricky he did not know. He said she should go to the warehouse by the airport – there was plenty that you could get there wholesale and cheap, jewellery, scarves, whatever.

Then you will not have to sit all day in the sun, he said, and he picked up her magnifier and held it against his face to make a giant's eye.

And it was at the wholesale store, in a scabby retail park near Málaga Airport, that she met Frédérique, who ran the place, and you had to stress the lavish q sound, which forced the mouth into a queasy smile. Frédérique was large and buttery and some kind of trans-sex – it was hard to tell which direction from which – and had a line on all the rackets. The wholesale place was a kind of front. It was peopled day and night by cirrhotic-looking old crooks and wastrel youths with insane mouths. These are my people, was Dilly Hearne's feeling. Soon she was living in the exurban sprawl of Málaga, and she was in Frédérique's place daily, and the cops were in and out too, and were on a first-name basis. There were many rackets and games. The money now was in the movement of people. Everybody came from elsewhere. Frédérique, when deep in her cups and on the burn of the pipe – late at night – would tell Dilly stories of the place that she came from. It was in the rainforest of Brazil. It was not two dozen miles, she said, from a tribe of seven families who'd never seen cars or electric light. Dilly imagined for a long time these happy Indians. She was like a kid seeking comfort in a story. She saw their yellow eyes burning electric in the gloom of the jungle by night, and heard the whispered prayer of their incantations, and now the low murmur of a great river is moving unseen, but nearby and – listen – how the unnameable birds shriek against the dark.

*

If she speaks to the men, it will mean the end of something. She goes outside for a smoke. There is a disturbance on the atmosphere. The air is tight and charged. She should leave this place at once and never look back. But she wants to speak to them.

Under the arclights a pack of Moroccan boys kick a ball around the wasteground by the container stacks. The ugly façades of the apartment blocks loom beyond the glow of the harbour lights. It is a plain sister of a town. Dilly passes through here often, and this much she has learned – the uglier the town, the kinder the people.

A helicopter of the narco police homes in across the water and hovers above the pad on the roof of the terminal and holds a moment, then softly drops, rests. It's very calming to watch this – she can feel her pulse rate slow with the blades.

She looks out across the water. She has not yet been told which hotel to stay in when she gets to Tangier. She awaits the instruction from Frédérique.

She tosses the smoke and tries to go back inside, but she has to approach the automatic door three times before it recognises her as womankind.

She keeps close to the walls as she examines the concourse, the ticket hatches. She takes the escalator upstairs. From the corner of her eye as she rises she keeps an eye on the men. Their unmistakable gaatch. Their mien. They look right through her again and she realises now that they cannot see her.

They are looking for some ghost called Dilly.

*

Something else that she had learned – you need to watch yourself at every minute of the day. If you don't watch yourself, the badness might slide in, or the evil. Watch your words most of all. Watch for the glamorous sentence that appears from nowhere – it might have plans for you. Watch out for the clauses that are elegantly strung, for the string of words bejewelled. Watch out for ripe language – it means your words may be about to go off.

And sometimes she could feel herself turning into someone else – into something else – and she came up from her meagre sleep in the Spanish night (maybe in Blanes, maybe in Calanda, maybe in Cabo de Gata) to hear her mother calling for one of the dogs on a lost lane on Beara long ago. The dog's name faded away before she could catch it – was it Shortie around that time?

She could not control the images that came through on the sleepless nights. She was from a line of insomniacs twelve hundred years long. She would never go back there, but home would always be the place where the light came slant at equinoctial times, in the half-seasons.

We were really so very far from the sun.

*

She watches them from above – two men on a bench, one with a good eye, and one with a good leg. She cannot go to them. Even if she could speak to them, what would she say?

That I cannot blame you any more.

When she was a child, there would be callers at strange hours. Men in hats, and laughing women, and sometimes there were raised voices, and sometimes singing. All the lurchy moves and late-night exits – we've got to do the splits again, Dilly, will you pack what you need in your dinosaur bag?

She can see her mother, in the hotel bed – in the old Jurys on the Western Road – and Cynthia pretends that she's asleep – for the child's sake – but she's turning again and again in a hot, awful soak, and she can feel the heat off her, it radiates, she's like a brick oven, and Maurice sits by the window, it's very late, it's summer and such a humid night, and he's looking out to the car park, smoking a number, and very lowly, under his breath, he's going

fuck fuck fuck fuck fuck fuck fuck fuck fuck fuck

and she knew then that they were definitely not like other families.

And Charlie Red would bring her to restaurants for her dinner and everyone seemed to move around them in circles, tighter and tighter circles around them, drawn in, as if they were dazzled or mesmerised, and people would come up out of nowhere and just grip his hand – Charlie Redmond! – and always he'd bring her for dinner, or for cakes and tea – it felt like escaping when she was with Charlie – and he'd give her sips of his wine, and tell her all of his old jokes again, and do all his voices, and buy her ridiculous, expensive things, and he'd whisper to her, he'd say, Dilly?

You're a fucking aristocrat.

And I loved you very much.

*

It is night at the port of Algeciras. The ferry is to sail again for Tangier. The crowd moves in spurts and gaggles towards the terminal gates. The two men on the bench survey the crowd carefully. The girl stands at a height above them. She leans on the balustrade and looks down. She needs to make a decision. But she is a prisoner of the past and the past will not relent. She remembers fucking everything. She remembers even that morning when the century was soon to turn, and Maurice took her in the car to the place by the water beyond the sleeping town of Berehaven, and the sound that was made – the resounding *shlunk* and *click* – when he locked all the doors, and even at four years old she knew what the dreadful look on his face was made of, it was made out of love.

Chapter Ten

THE GESTURE WOUND

In the cities of Cádiz, Barcelona, Segovia and Málaga,
and at the port of Algeciras, from 2000 to 2004

But yes Ireland closes in like a motherfucker. It turns its
crooked mouth in the darkness and whispers of the bad
things. It picks its moment and shows the hornèd claws. He
fled from it a few weeks after the century turned – Maurice
Hearne was not Y2K compliant, was his serious opinion. He
had almost killed his girl. He had lost his wife. He had
knifed his friend. Death was nearby – he was certain; he felt
the whisper of its breath – and he pelted from it. He went
to Spain because it was a country vast and made for hiding.
He would be lost to it for a long time.

*

He roamed the place mindlessly. He tried to coax a pattern
from his days, but there was no pattern. He drank like a
bastard. He talked to the walls. He gave out to the policía.
He got into bad, bad fights. He shot up between his toes.

He was in Spain for the brittle greys of its Februarys, the St John's yellow of its vaulting Junes. He did not take up the language. He was among the wynds of the white cities and the hollows and the bars of the sombre towns. He was lost to the true dark of the Spanish plain by night. He was aboard the train that stopped at every small country station. His loneliness was all of his own making.

For almost five years he drifted in Spain in this way. He was a young man still, but he did not feel young at all. He ran from the hard-faced gaatch of himself. The sense elements that were most vivid –

the chemical tang on the wind that came across the beach by night in Tarifa

the cathedral stone that was hot to the touch in the evening sun of Salamanca

the migraine whine of gathered voices above the café bar at the estación de autobuses in Granada

– did not amount to a consciousness of that time but made the textures for it only. He had no grip at that time. He moved on the breeze.

For a while it was in the city of Cádiz that the morning light found his pale skin, the wet film of his eyes, the knit bones of his face. He lived with skinny Karima in the old town there.

*

The fish smell of the market was heavy on the air. Tiny opaque scales and twisted fish bones were everywhere on the streets and in the gutters. The fish blood and its ripe iron smell stirred notions of sexual abandon. He was still in a condition of hopeless lust. He was tormented, flailing, cuntstruck. Karima was forty-seven to his thirty-three and she would fuck half the night away – it was exhausting, exultant, terrific stuff. Karima couldn't go within a hundred miles of Málaga or certainly she would be killed. She had bad sweats when she slept and so she slept rarely. She fried him sparrows in the mornings. The shapes of the birds were still evident on the brown chipped delf. The scraps of meat were fragrant in the garlicky oil and gamey.

Karima knew old magic. Strange breezes moved across her features. Unreadable glazes emerged from deep within her face. Sometimes in the course of the act she took his hand and guided his fingers to her arsehole. She made it so that she quivered.

To recover, he sat in the square and drank red wine in the late mornings, and he had long, hard chats with himself. The flags of the Guardia Civil blew sharply above the barrack house and snapped in the Atlantic wind. He wrote mad letters to his wife (full of screeched insinuations), and to his daughter (whispers of love), but immediately he ripped and binned them.

*

He rented the apartment from a yapping Scotsman with a poodle's face. He was an ex-polis who talked out ceaselessly the plot of a gory thriller he would never write – a killer's lair, a stack of blood-encrusted animal pelts, a rusty creak of the trapdoor's hinge. What was wrong with people? That

155

was what Maurice Hearne wanted to know. The world in the new century had slipped into a sordid haze. It was dying of vulgarity. This was his considered opinion. As well as the fucking he was masturbating as much as thrice in the day.

The days moved past like sentences, the nights.

And Karima turned – as he knew that she would – and she started to make bad magic for him. She put her spells on him. She wanted all his money or what was left of it. She was out of the business. She had a number on her back. There was a tentful of gaunt brothers pegged high on the Rif to send the money back to.

She hid strange packages among the plants in the apartment. Clumps of dog hair; bird bones; dried herbs tied up in bundles; once, hysterically, a hen's foot. He woke in the night to find her crouched on her knees above his chest and muttering darkly. These were not nights without event. He whispered his own cold words to her loins, her belly.

This was in the city of Cádiz, where the people are Gaditano.

This was in Andalusia, in the springtime of 2000.

She told him lots of old stories – she told stories about her father.

Once, in the port of Algeciras, the policía had brought her father to the barrack house and unlocked a cabinet full of confiscated weapons and told him to take his pick – it was his best chance to get out of the town alive. Rows of machetes and long knives gleamed under the strip lights – there were knuckle-dusters too, and pointed shivs of stainless steel with hooked handles. The native weaponry was ingenious as this was a Catholic place.

Fathers throw the longer shadows. We get over the mothers, at last, but hardly ever the fathers, she said.

In Cádiz he drifted on the bone-iron smell of the fish market and he was assailed by images of sexual fury. In fact, he more or less got used to them. Which was the dangerous thing.

He drank and fucked and ranted. He slept little by night. He was living in the amalgam place of a dream. Cities turned into other cities; streets turned into distant streets. Karima's kisses tasted of oil and smoke.

They fucked each other also in the mornings. He found on most mornings the strange packages hidden among the house plants. Chivalrous yet, he disposed of them without remark. He felt it was possible that she might try to poison him.

Oh, but the dusted brown of her irises was a very beautiful tone – it was a nutty Saharan brown as of a wind-blown dune or a crested lark.

They told each other in the darkness their dreams and nightmares of the Barbary Coast.

*

Karima killed the football from the Bernabéu on the TV set and kicked the wall and announced that they were to break up. No explanations. He fell to his knees and declared tearfully that he loved her and his Cork accent had never been more pronounced.

She hit him a dig in the face.

The salt of blood all sexy on his lips.

She started to fling his stuff from the balcony, marching back and forth, with her vivacious cheekbones, her killer's mouth.

Not my fucken records, babe, he said.

She dragged him from the room. She had the strength of a fucking stallion. She smashed the door shut after him.

Ah, calm the fuck down, Reem, wouldn't you?

But he was talking to the bricks. The picture disintegrated. Now Maurice Hearne was stood up on the street in the rain in his shirtsleeves. Karima continued to fling his belongings from on high.

Not the fucken vinyl!

He tried to catch them as they spun through the air.

Karima! There's fucken years gone into them records!

He stood in the evening on the street in the haze of rainflecked light. The backfire of a fucked moto cracked like a gunshot, but he did not flinch from it. He had more on his plate.

Karima on the balcony with flashing teeth assailed him. She called him a liar, a whoremaster, a faggot.

The vinyl smashed all around him.

Notes cracked open on the pavement.

In Cádiz that year our love was volatile.

Attraction that slithers towards the cusp of homicide.

Karima called him a coward, a yellow rat, a cunt.

Darkness rimmed the sky west above the ramparts and the ocean.

The Atlantic birds squalled in murderous packs like home.

But at least now he had a sense of himself. This was without question an event. A dangerous woman in a fitted black dress raged from a balcony in a sidestreet of Cádiz. The way that her long, needle limbs flexed and the overbite of her white teeth was cinema – the teeth were a vampire's incisors.

Now he stood with his hands on his hips blithely as his stuff landed on the stones of the street all around him.

Cádiz breathed low and calmly like a waiting serpent.

Karima? Go handy on yourself, wouldn't you?

She raged for a while yet on the balcony. The rain fell; the moments tumbled; the air was ripe and funky after Carnaval.

Karima ran down her batteries at last. Now she was draped over the edge of the balcony, exhausted, and he knew that she might turn back to love quickly.

Down the way –

The vagrant youth beat their drums and biscuit boxes on
the rainy beach and smoked hashish, and the girls and the
dogs laughed and barked at the stars and rain.

This was in the city of Cádiz, back in 2000, on the coast of
light and magic.

*

It was in Plaça de Catalunya that he first met Remick. She
was dark also and from Australia. She attached herself to
him like a drugged wombat. He took her to a bar he used to
own in the '90s on a sidestreet of L'Eixample. He displayed
the place with a seigneurial flourish. It had cleaned money
for him and then he sold it again. The trays of anchovies
were laid out still in green oil flecked with garlic. The
streets ran into the same streets. He was down to about
nine thousand by now. He sat with lovely Remick at the
same table he'd always used down back. She had a smile
like a home-made explosive device. It did not travel to her
eyes.

He said, Remick, I could say things to you in the night that
you would never fucking recover from.

They lived together for a while in the district of Gràcia.
They drank too much and too late. They fought with
venom and skill. They smoked rock cocaine. They fought
like drunk gorillas. Gràcia was not what it had been even
five years previously. There was no longer good heroin.
Now there were stores that sold specialist honey – 'The
flower of the mountain'. The new century was a fucking

atrocity. He belonged to the previous one. Small elegant dogs waddled in their coats in the Catalan winter sun. Remick headbutted him one morning – she had the manners of a fucken sheep-shearer – and then they made love again. He saw the stars of heaven when he came.

He was followed everywhere by two Moroccan boys.

He saw them night and day.

They lurked around the edges of the square in Gràcia.

The boys were lank and twentyish.

He was certain that Karima had sent them.

Are they looking this way, Remick? Is all I'm fucken asking you.

But I can't see who you're talking about!

Two fucken Maroc!

I don't see anybody.

Ah, open your eyes and fucken look, would you?

He spun quickly in the café and maybe caught a flash of them darting to the shadows outside. This was what you were dealing with. Everywhere he walked he could feel their Riffian eyes between his shoulder blades like fucking knives. Here was another place he would need to take his leave of – Barcelona, in 2003.

*

He began to lose the ability to speak to people. He was out of his language too long. He was losing his words. This was in a city of the interior. This was in the lyric winter of Segovia. He loved Dilly and Cynthia. He could not see them. Outside the internet café a gypsy kid and his girl sold punnets of chestnuts from a roasting cart and kissed. They looked like the year 1583. The air was dark blue and had the smoke of old poetry at dusklight. He no longer pretended that the cheerful words he scratched down on the back of a card would be sent to his daughter. He could no longer imagine how her face might have changed. He sat at the café window and looked out to the winding street that rose to the cathedral plaza. On a search engine he found images of the Ummera Wood: a ghost of sunflare through a faded Irish place. The odour of its melancholy. He ripped up the postcard.

He went in dreams inevitable to the old wood of the Ummera in north Cork.

His first years were spent there with a suffering father and a stoical mother. His father was from further west, from the bone and treeless hills of Beara. At the Ummera his father was unsettled by the trees. This was his mother's belief. There were strange pulses like worms at the base of the father's throat. In Segovia the church bells clanged the sombre notes of the hour, the half-hour, the quarter. They laid it on thick enough still around these places. His father had been a great religious. When they moved to Cork city, his father got involved with the Charismatics. He was all but carried home from the meetings. Fainting fits. Speaking-in-tongues. His father also would lose the gist of his sentences. He would lose track of them at the knuckle and turn. There were strange olden words on his lips as he slept in the afternoons. Maurice as a boy watched him, and then as a teenager, as the condition worsened, and in Segovia he felt the impress yet of his father's unresting spirit.

He felt older than his time. He feared his own reflection in the lit windows of the Spanish evening. He believed there was age gone onto him. His face had a sunken look. He could make out his own skull in it. He felt the worms in his mouth. His body was a cavern of death. He was thirty-six years to fucken Jesus. (He felt with a cool certainty that he'd be dead by thirty-seven.) He went to a bar on Calle Marqués del Arco and ate fried fish and thin slices of jamón ravenously and drank the inky rioja and cold beer from the tap and wept openly and nobody paid any attention to him at all. A fat blind child sang on a TV talent show and the bar was agog and the patrons began to clap along with the song – it was a Spanish translation of an old Carpenters' number, and all of the child's chins rolled. Maurice Hearne was so moved that a seep of vomit rose up in his throat. He stuffed a heel of bread down his throat to tamp it.

The note in Segovia that winter was tragi-comical, capricious, beautiful.

*

South again on the drag of the old sea. The beach at Malagueta was the same as ever it was. Spidery old men and poor brown boys fished from the rocks at the eastern end. It was a hot clean spring. Grand villas loomed expressively on the hills above. Hunting birds hovered on the thermal air.

Hale ancient Germans walked the promenade in the sun. Maurice lay down on a boulder of the seabreak. He was a crab at bask in the springtime sun. There were moments of odd, steely belief – he believed that he could get Cynthia back, and Dilly.

The heat was religious. There were dark rumours in the channels of his body. Surly runners went the length of the prom in steadfast pairs. He listened to the old working city of Málaga and its Catholic bells, its Catholic silences. He squinted to take in the expanse above.

Oh, look at the white blue sky above me now – should I address my confessions to it?

He lay a long while on the boulder, until the heat of the sun diminished and the cool of evening came down again like a lowered veil, a kindness.

In Málaga the evening streets played the same old woozy music still. Hooded eyes on these streets like trapdoors. Cowls of monks and sad little nuns. He sat on the single bed of a room in a pension off Calle Larios. He listened to the drone of the evening paseo, its gossip and murmurs. He rested his eyes. He drank Cruzcampo beer from small tins and pissed his looks down the sink. He felt the worms tunnelling beneath his eyes.

Right on fucken cue, he said aloud.

The past shifted and rearranged itself. He could not step out from its reach. The past was fluid in the moment. He addressed a few casual remarks to his father even. Then the not-so-casual –

I thought I was so much stronger than you.

Does expression – cold, plain, pure – does it ever find its way through? He was a man no longer quite young pissing in a sink in a thirty-five-euro room in Málaga. With the arch betrayer in his fucking hand. Expression enough.

He went out to the night and drank with the Algerians in a dockside bar. He needed to organise a shipment again. He believed it was doable. He had made contact with Charlie Redmond. There was a definite thaw. He liked the softness of the Algerians' quiet, conspiratorial talk. He hadn't an iota what they were saying to each other. He wished to be made clean in harsh sealight in a place that did not know his name.

His father's spells had made the world sway and lean in. When Maurice was a child, his father was taken frequently to the hospital. The stays became longer and longer. His mother explained it all plainly and without emotion.

Maurice read up on it. Electrodes, he learned, would be attached at points to his father's head. By this means, electricity was passed through in neat measures to stimulate the brain. Brief seizures were induced. He saw the doctors recede from the room and into blue sky as the anaesthetic took hold. New connections were established in the hippocampus.

But if his father's mood was steadier when he returned home from hospital, there was also an odd grey calm that possessed him. It was from another world. It broke up all the sleep in the house.

Málaga eased into its night hours. There was a liner due in from Genoa. The prostitutes arrived on the hoot of its bass-toned call. The bar would be open the length of the night. Maurice Hearne was happy enough to sit quietly on the crest of his old sad dreams.

*

At the port of Algeciras the criminal despondency of half Europe had gathered. The air had a medieval tang. The vagrant children of many nations were crouched and high and drunken there. All the drums and the girls and the dogs were arrayed. Tiny fires showed against the dark as the pipes were drawn on. The atmosphere was of solemn ceremony. These were often quite humourless children. The port by night had a hot, diabolic quality. It rang of the past but was of the new century. On such a clear night you could see an hour south to the lamps of Tangier.

He went to walk the hours of his waiting through the old port streets. Strange hawks watched darkly from the alleyways. It was one of the unsolvable places of the earth. As he moved, he felt watched over or filmed. He felt also like he was closing in on something. He waited for the night crossing across the black water. What was left of the money was hidden in small wads about his person. He had to get his women back.

When the call for the night boat at last came, it dragged the world back to an older frame. The footsteps that moved over the dockside stones and the gangplank had the certain reminiscence of war. Across an easy water the boat moved. The waves went regularly as troops beneath. The ferry made a jaunty, marching music. He moved out for Tangier with no plan. The night was quick and black around him.

The next morning at a pension in the Arab quarter of that fatal city he opened his left eye with a razor blade.

Chapter Eleven

THE LAST NIGHT OF OUR ACQUAINTANCE

Leaving the port of Algeciras, in October 2018

From the ferry boat the lights of Algeciras recede into the October night. The dark mountains above the town are getting smaller. The fortress of Gibraltar is lost behind a cloudbank. Somewhere in the distance a thunderstorm crackles. Dilly's phone throbs once and she reaches for it and a text from Frédérique names the hotel in Tangier she is to go to – it's the El Muniria again. That is all she needs – she throws the phone into the water. Fuck your roaming charges and fuck your bundle rates.

Piercing the black, the searchlight of a narco chopper rakes the sky above the Straits.

There is a great heaviness on the air – a tension that makes the breath catch in her throat – and the stars tonight are not visible. There is a cool breeze off the water. The thunderstorm comes nearer as an electric wafting.

Hard smokers line the rails on the top deck – the Moroccans are unquenchably the greatest smokers on the planet, and Dilly lights up among them. These silent travellers in harried conversation with themselves. The music inside plays off the beat.

Now as the boat moves out further Algeciras goes to slow black.

When you are twenty-three years old, there are moments when your life is just a film. She peels off her skin and throws it to the water. This winter she will not come back from Maroc. Maybe she'll go to Essaouira for a season and find a boy or find a girl. Get some dogs of her own at last.

And picture for me now a slight girl with cropped hair running with the dogs on a winter beach by night – she is gamine; her movement is fleet – and when she calls out to the dogs, her voice is musical, lilting, and still quite Irish, actually.

On the night boat to Tangier she can let the past recede. In the terminal she walked right by the men as they scanned the crowd and with defiance she turned her face to them. To speak with the men would have been to step back through a screen she had with three years of hard time erected.

The black water breaks up and reforms again perfectly as the boat passes through.

The Moroccans smoke and drink bottles of Mahou beer, and now, as Tangier begins to show as a low rim of lights on the southern dark, they talk lowly among themselves.

Down here it is a mean century. It will disintegrate further. Dilly has enough money to pull away from Frédérique now. The night boat arrows a straight course across the sea. There is a sense of military advance, an army's passage.

She goes inside and descends clankily the iron steps to the ferry's lounge, and she is aware of the glances that she draws as she goes by. She displays her face in a particular way and nobody but nobody approaches the slight girl with the bleached and cropped hair.

In the early morning she will sit on the terrace at the El Muniria and have coffee and pastries with the camp old Englishmen who stay there always. She may have to wait for three days, she may have to wait for four. Stoic hours. The light will be brilliant with the storm passed over, the air pure and clear. She will hear the muezzin call above the medina and see the great birds hover on the white seafront at evening.

Now breathe, and step out again, a step further from the past.

Step into the streets as narrow as bones, the white streets of the labyrinth, and breathe deeply.

Breathe, and step out once more.

*

Do you think it was definitely not her, Maurice?

I'm certain of it, Charlie.

All that's wrong with us, Moss? We been staring into the mass of fucken humanity for so long, our minds are playing tricks.

Our deranged little minds are acting up. Is all that's wrong with us, Charles.

For half a minute, though?

Stop.

I halfways thought . . .

I had a strong suspicion too, Charlie. There was a kind of . . . I don't know. A gaatch to it?

I felt kind of . . .

Yeah.

Like my legs, like they were . . .

I couldn't fucken breathe, Charlie. Being quite honest with you. I still can't breathe. I'm put me on a fucken drip material.

She fucken . . .

The way she turned and looked right through us, Charlie?

A coldness, kind of . . . Whoever she was.

Definitely it might not have been her.

Definitely I think it wasn't her. It's just our . . .

I'm certain. I mean we're so long in this fucken place now?

Hallucinations. Is where we're at, Moss. It's sorrowful, really.

The little maggoty brains are playing up.

Even if it was her, Maurice?

Yeah?

There's no fear of the girl.

No. She's going to be fine.

My heart is going like a fucken greyhound, Moss.

I know.

You could tie me down and sedate me.

Don't mention the sedation, Charlie. I've fucken been there. I don't ever want to go under again. Not ever.

A troubled silence descends – the old times are shifting again; they are rearranging like fault lines.

The past will not relent.

Chapter Twelve

IT'S MOVIE NIGHT AT THE BUGHOUSE

In the city of Cork, in April 2013

It was one of those hectic April mornings that has the eyes screwed wrong in your head. There was too much busyness on the air. Maurice Hearne had been put out of the Beara house, and she had tried to turn Dilly against him – the old one-two, and he was too weak for it now.

Quickly he had come loose of himself. He could feel the new season in hard pulses in the glands. On the larches (primly erect, arrogant as surgeons) that lined the avenue to the Psychiatric the buds were rudely swollen – he couldn't take his eyes off them, they were like fucken nipples. It's tricky, always, when the world is coming to life again.

His mother, Cissie, led him by the arm through the grounds of the old Victorian hospital. They had suffered a week of it together. Days of tears and rage; nights of froth and demon visions; the works. They had taken a taxi out to the strange place, but he did not recall the ride that had ended just a minute previously. They could have been driven out there by an aardvark for all he knew.

As they walked, his mother shushed him and cajoled. The bird-like pursing of her lips worked up tiny wet sucks – he'd choke her, on the spot, if he had the strength – and her sighs opened pockets of woe in the cold, bright air.

The ground was waking, and opening: there was a high mustiness like yeast. Gay white flowers tossed back their heads like show ponies. He was under referral to the Psychiatric at his mother's insistence.

Come on, Moss, there's no fault in you, boy.

Shut the fucken gob, Ma, would ya?

These were the mean times. Cynthia said no more, no more. Dilly had turned into a compost heap. He had not talked to Charlie Redmond for a couple of years. There were those who wanted him dead still.

The sun came through the larches in thin, white slants, and his mother relaxed into a state of deep relief – he felt her grip on his arm slacken – as she led him up the stone steps and through the heavy doors.

The Mental.

The Bin.

The Bughouse.

In the consultant's waiting room, like a child, he held his mother's hand for solace.

*

He was more than possessed by his crimes and excesses – he was the gaunt accumulation of them. He wanted an out, but he could never be a suicide. He could not willingly deprive the world of himself. He was almost forty-six and if fate did not intervene, he would have to sit it the fuck out.

The consultant was of a type for these places – a squat and antic old time-server who looked madder than Napoleon.

Arrange your face, doctor, Maurice said.

Ah, now, Moss, his mother said.

The consultant shaped his lips in an amused pursing.

Forgive me, father, for I have sinned, Maurice said. It's been twenty-eight days since my last chicken supper.

He could hear what the dogs could hear. He could make as much sense of it. He could smell the tiniest things – he could smell the stale leather of the soles of the consultant's ox-blood brogues.

You're possibly experiencing agitation, Mr Hearne? At the moment?

Am I the fuck, he said.

Maurice, his mother said, your tongue.

It's all right, Mrs Hearne.

Delicately, with the tips of his fingers, the consultant lifted a form from the desk.

Are you prepared to sign the committal, Maurice?

I'm prepared to hop up on the committal's back, Maurice said, and give it a pet name.

This is more of the nonsense talk, doctor. You're confused, Mossie. Don't mind the auld talk, would you?

He scratched out the letters on the form with a prideful flourish. He held the form out in front of his face and he considered the two scrawled words at arm's length – these were the sum facts of himself.

You'll get a grand rest now, Cissie said. You won't know yourself, Maurice.

You want me to spell out my disease, doctor?

Ah, Moss . . .

H.E.A.R.N.E.

*

Three days' sedation was the first course of the treatment but he was wired so fiercely it was difficult to stay under. He came and went from himself in an off-white room. He was afloat on a kind of sea. Once, he awoke with the startling realisation that he was a criminal – it was the first time in his life he had considered himself as such.

But he could see the first swallows of the year darting across the patch of sky outside, drawing out their fast, invisible threads, and these, he knew, were holding the world together.

*

Slowly, as the days passed and the chemicals were reduced, he emerged from a heavy, dreaming state to a calmer and more wakeful one. The years had leaned into years, one into the next. He had been in and out of his marriage; his love had not reduced. He had bought fourteen apartments in Budapest and sold them at a tremendous loss. He had mislaid, with Charlie Redmond, a tonne and a half of Moroccan hashish. It was never found. He had been in and out with Charlie too. The seasons were relentless; the years turned over. It was a fucking joke life. It was fucking beautiful. They never caught us – that was the important thing.

He became aware now, a little to the west of himself, of a voice – it was an old, countryish voice – and he realised after some time that it was actual, not internal, and that it was from the bed beside his. There were just two beds to the room and, when he had the strength to turn to the other, he did so, and he saw there the bulky, prone figure of what looked to be an old farmer type.

Some misfortune netted from the hills of the county, Maurice guessed, who had listened to the rain too insistently, maybe, until he took his instructions from the voices within it.

The old man lay on a pillow sodden with drool, and his eyes were drawn to the patch of pale sky, its meagre light, and he made words on his cracked lips, accusations, it sounded like.

If I hadn't enough on my plate, thought Maurice Hearne, and he felt for the old man.

*

Over these April days, as his strength returned, as he began to eat boiled eggs at four in the afternoon and drink mugs of strong tea, Maurice was able to lift himself from the bed and join the procession – at last, inevitably – of the green corridor, and it wasn't entirely joyless, he found, to be able to drag one foot after the other, and to have no sense of a war inside.

This time it had been worse than in '99; it had been worse even than in 2004, when he opened the eye in Tangier. But now he came up to himself slowly again – it was like rising through heavy water – and he was warmed by one of the great consolations: nothing very terrible lasts for very long.

*

The farmer recovered too. After a couple of days he sat up in the bed and asked for tea and the Examiner. These old coves read their own weather so closely – there was a quiet satisfaction about the farmer's mouth that showed he knew the tempest had passed over. They began to talk to each other.

Kiwi fruits, the old man said, confidentially.

Go again?

Kiwi fruits, the farmer said, be your only man for the mental.

That right?

I read it in the paper. Scientists have discovered. One a day keep you right in yourself good as the tablets.

The farmer was dispatched to the free world before Maurice was, which said something about fucking something. He walked the green corridor. His mother chattily visited, and it was as though nothing had happened, as though together on these recent nights they hadn't been around the rings of Saturn. He spoke to Cynthia by phone.

You'll be fine, she said. It's just the time for it, you know? It's time for you to be on your own now, Maurice.

Can I see the girl? he said, and she did not answer.

One morning, after a long, dreamless sleep, he woke to find a new neighbour installed in the bed beside his, a long, thin figure turning angrily in a drugged fugue.

It was Charlie Redmond.

*

Of course you could pump the River Ganges' worth of lithium into Charlie Red and there'd be no keeping him down.

Maurice watched – with the old fond amusement – as Charlie got up out of the bed, paced the room like a single human shriek made flesh and bone, the eyes out on

181

stalks, the face bloodless and intense, the knees climbing up and down the walls, and the arseless gown flapping after him. The attending Nightingale was in and out with her hopeless pleading, trying to get him back in the bed again.

Trust her, Charlie, she's a nurse.

But if Charlie Red was there, also he was not yet there. His eyes were open, but they had no recognition in them; he looked at Maurice sometimes in his waking fits but as a visitation only.

He looked at him as if it were the ghost of Banquo in the bed farside of him.

*

Maurice kept watch as slowly his broken friend emerged from the fog, and he was there to present a sly smile when Charlie's eyes flickered open to focus truly.

Are you a pillow-over-the-face job, Charles?

Moss?

I'm here for you, old pal. And I think I might have the strength back in me arms for it.

*

As in the slow push-in of a zoom, the days came into focus. The nights in their own way clarified. The men found a way into their talk again, and fraternity.

How you doing big-picture wise, Maurice?

I'm fucked up, Charles. Yourself?

Shockin' condition altogether.

They talked against the boredom and fear. They took their meds with gusto – here come the happy tray, Charlie Redmond said – and they avoided the television room.

Telly room'd depress the fucken Jesus out of you, Maurice said.

Telly room, you'd be stringin' yourself up, Charlie said.

We could get a laptop brought in, Charlie? Internet dongle? Watch shit?

A laptop? I'm watchin' me fucken shoes in this place, Moss.

*

They had a laptop brought in. They streamed some old stuff. They lay back into a soak of nostalgia. These were slow nights at the Bughouse. The long stretch of the April evenings was a cruel sentence. They watched Rumble Fish again.

They had watched it when they were sixteen or seventeen, until the tape had worn thin on the VHS and the footage went snowy, a monochrome dream of violence, death and helpless brotherhood, the Motorcycle Boy and Rusty James, and the lights of Tulsa were coldly burning, and their own world could be redrawn to its dimensions.

*

They sold dope up and down Barrack Street. 1983. 1984. It was bought wholesale from a family of nine brothers off an estate in Mahon. All nine brothers went by the name of Sox. Maurice and Charlie stashed their dope behind the cross on the deadhouse wall, under the bonnet of an abandoned car on Evergreen Street, beneath the kneeling cushion of a confession box. They were in and out of the church so often the priest started to lock it up weekday evenings.

Pray at home, he told the wailing widowers, the grievously sick, the unnaturally morose.

There were money and supply difficulties with the brothers named Sox. There were talk-to-the-fucken-dog situations erupting. Maurice and Charlie made a connection with a soldier at Collins Barracks. The soldiers were in and out of the Lebanon on peace-keeping missions and flew home unsearched. Maurice and Charlie were soon taking delivery of nine-ounce bars of soft, sandy Lebanese hashish.

You didn't even put your lighter to it, Moss.

The way it just crumbled into the skins, Charlie? Gorgeous.

The Lebanese blond on Barrack Street was the finest to be had in town. Trouble stirred accordingly. Hateful dogs were produced; crow bars; knives. Charlie Redmond was arranged in the boot of a car and driven to a field beyond Kanturk.

That was the night that put hairs on me chest, he said, as they ate boiled eggs together at the Bughouse.

184

Money accrued; ambition was fed. Dope brought girls and money. There was languor by day and violence in the night.

*

Dilly was allowed to visit. She sat in her motley array and dreadlocks, and she twisted the tips of the locks, and looked up.

But in the same fucking room? she said.

Her little posh accent was heart-breaking.

As fate and fortune would arrange it, Dill.

Me and your old man, Dilly? It's a written-in-the-stars-type number.

We're thinking of running away with each altogether, Maurice said.

We could open a bar in Tenerife, Moss. We might be very happy down there. Hang out our sign. Dancing tonight.

She looked from one to the other and back again. She gathered into a bundle of herself, drew up her legs – Dilly had a complicated arrangement with furniture always, and she took a while to settle. She wore her weather on the tip of her nose. Happiness brought a moment's dim blushing there; the tip whitened visibly if she were scared, and she was scared right now.

This place? Maurice said, as he saw her despair. It's not as bad as they make out, Dilly.

Give us another week, Charlie said, we'll be running the joint.

And I mean we're rattlin' with happy pills.

Serious tack they're serving, girl. There's matinee and evening performances up and down that corridor.

But the same room? she said.

An arrayal of the stars, Maurice said. How's your mother, girl?

Ah, she's you know.

I do, yeah.

Dilly played with the tips of her braided locks, twisted one and turned it, chewed on it a moment, tucked her legs beneath herself again. She considered the men, in their twin beds, in their baby-blue gowns, with their slack, tranquillised mouths and desperate eyes, and she could not but smile, the tip of her nose softly reddening.

In my opinion? Charlie said. Bob Marley should have gone and lopped the big toe off himself altogether.

He'd still be alive today, Maurice said. He'd be bouncin' around the place.

You see it was on account of the Rastafarian beliefs, Dilly, that he wouldn't have the toe lopped off. And the infection spread and that's all she wrote.

I have a mild case of dreadlocks, Dilly said. I don't have Rastafarian beliefs. And actually I'm not that into Bob. Though I suppose I kind of like 'Duppy Conqueror'.

Too cool for school, Maurice said. Who else you listening to?

I don't know . . . Lee Scratch Perry?

Never heard of him, Charlie said. Or hang about? He's not a butcher's apprentice from Mayfield, is he?

That's him, yeah.

How you getting on with the old God business lately, Dill?

Not something I think about much, Da.

You had a bit of a spell for a while, though, didn't you?

Very briefly. I got past it.

Wait till they get you in the likes of this place, Maurice said. Can find your mind turning in spiritual-type directions at all hours.

See that payphone out in the corridor? Charlie said. You put fifty cent in that, you get three minutes with the Big Man. It's a special rate for the supernaturally afflicted.

You been onto him, Charlie?

I'm onto him morning and night, girl. Have you any change?

What's he been saying to you?

Says he's missing an angel.

Fuck off, Charlie.

They settled into it together. They arranged the laptop on a chair between the two beds and she sat back on the edge of Maurice's and they watched Rumble Fish again.

In my humble and honest? Maurice said. We could be looking at Francis Ford Coppola's finest hour.

You mean like Sofia's da? Dilly said.

The men traded a painful glance.

She don't even know these actors, Charlie said. But, actually, looking at it again . . . Is it me or was I something like a Matt Dillon-type in my younger days?

You were the bulb off him, Charlie. But come here. Have you seen Mickey Rourke lately?

Think I saw him on the number eight going up MacCurtain Street. Top-right-hand seat, overhead the driver.

He's after leaving himself go something shockin'.

He is, yeah. They nearly had to turf him off the number eight.

*

Maurice walked her out the corridor and he laid his arm about her thin shoulder.

I want no more of this Spain talk, he said.

Da? I'm nearly eighteen.

I'd miss you, though.

Two tears in a bucket, Dilly said. Motherfuck it.

Dilly? I just want you to stay close for a while, you know? And come here . . . You know that I love you, don't you?

Ah, Da. Please? I mean, seriously?

I know, yeah. Okay.

*

These last days at the Bughouse. They lay in the twin beds beside each other, and, late one morning, a moment opened that allowed the words to be spoken –

You know I think the girl could be mine, Maurice? I mean there is a possibility.

I know there is, Charlie. I know that.

Chapter Thirteen

CYNTHIA AND DILLY – THE QUIET STORY

In Cork and on Beara, from April 2013 to August 2015

She walked with her mother through the April city. The birds were on fucking springs. Remorse was the lightness of her step, the relief that she was beyond the Bughouse walls.

That's one that'll stick to your bones, Cynthia said. I'm sorry you had to go through it. How are they looking?

Insane.

It'll do that for you, the Mental.

They're watching Rumble Fish . . .

Jesus Christ.

. . . and doing all the lines.

They don't get over themselves, do they?

No.

And the long fella lands himself in there how exactly?

An arrayal of the stars they're calling it.

Ah, they would do, yeah.

Fate and magic, et cetera.

If one of them doesn't strangle the other, Cynthia said, we can call it a result. They do fill a room, though, don't they?

They do, yes.

Is your father kind of wandery still?

How'd you mean?

I mean are his thoughts, you know . . . heading in strange directions?

It's Maurice. When are his thoughts fucking not? They're both kind of . . . I don't know. Tranked-looking? Pale.

Yeah, well, they're in the fucking Mental, aren't they? We'll go and eat a bun, will we?

They went to the Crawford. They ate carrot cake with fresh cream and drank Americanos. The fathomless ease of the faces all around them, and the nerveless chatter – no, we are not like other families. Dilly looked at her mother in a certain way; Cynthia lowered her cup, because there was a challenge in the look.

Did you ever see them violent?

Ah, Jesus, Dilly, please.

Did you?

Where's this coming from?

I don't know.

Why would you ask me something like that? No, I did not.

I don't believe you.

Believe what you fucking like.

Her mother's face made an attempt at a blank, unreadable glaze, but quickly the slyness of a grin tipped up the corners of her mouth.

Okay, she said.

Okay what?

Once I saw Maurice thump the head off some young fella on Washington Street.

When was this?

Oh, God, I don't know. It was, like . . . '93? '94? I remember it was outside the Pot Black Pool Hall.

The what?

Before your time.

And this was over drugs?

No . . . I believe something might have been said about his shoes.

His shoes?

As I recall.

And, like . . . very violent?

I suppose. It was kind of, you know . . . Bit sickening.

You watched it?

Well, I was fucking there. What could I do? It was horrible. Scary. And I remember his heart was just like thumping out of his chest for about an hour after it. And it was . . . oh, I don't know.

What?

It was a bit kind of horny as well. If I'm being honest with you.

Ah, Jesus Christ, Ma.

You asked me.

They went to the English Market. Everybody looked breezy and glad of themselves. Cynthia bought olives, monkfish and sourdough bread, some coffee beans and bulbs of fennel. The fennel was to settle her stomach. Her stomach lately was ripped and hysterical.

We'd want to leg it out the road before that fish starts talking to us, Dilly, she said.

They drove out the back road to Beara. The countryside was trying to shuck the last of the winter from its shoulders. Cynthia chewed on a piece of raw fennel and her aniseed breath scented the car. Is she still beautiful, Dilly wondered, with a wounded, sidelong glance. Certainly she had a skin tone that would make you puke it was so clear. She didn't look forty-one. She had nice, sad eyes. She had a mouth that was really fucking vivacious when she laughed, but she did not laugh much. Mostly she looked as if she were in a condition of vague disbelief about the world. As in what the hell are you going to throw at me next?

We've all been through a very great deal, Dilly said.

This is apropos of?

Apropos of my fucking hole.

*

There is a stab of awareness at the beginning and at the end of love, and the feeling precisely replicates – it's a twinge of cold certainty at either end of the affair, and it is twice terrifying. He would not be allowed back into the house again. The long war was at last over. The internecine strife of Maurice and Cynthia. More than twenty years she had given it. The sleeplessness and pain of the long absences, the hot lurches of emotion, the sudden reversals of fortune, the endless pleadings, the slow relentings, the golden times of morphiate heaven, the atrocities on both sides, the shock tactics, and the giddy joy of their lavish sexual reunions – it was all done with now. The summer came in slowly and gently and lit the peninsula. The gannets plunged to attack the new mackerel shoals. The clifftops were a riot of sea pinks, bird's-foot trefoil, ox-eye daisies. The Skelligs sat dreaming far off in the June haze. Cynthia expected a measure of peace, at last, but the truth was that she felt like the insides of a fucking dog.

*

Late in the night there were voices from the beach. She came up from the shallows of a thin, morbid sleep, and the thugs of her dreams were led away. Youth, or at least that season's faithful guild of it, came to play nightly on the beach. They drank and laughed and fucked each other on the back sands. By night the old shoreline was narcotic.

Cynthia put the bones of her feet to the floor and darkly muttered and went to the window. The new house, as she still thought of it, five years on – glass and steel and a view of the bay, built when they had been hog-fat, briefly, on the profits of Ard na Croí. It was from this place they were to see the gales come in. Here they were to drink little. They were to think not about the possibilities of heroin. Oh, Maurice, what did we do to each other?

In the dark glass now she caught her glance gauntly – Jesus, I'd really want to do something with my fucking eyes, wouldn't I? She turned from the image – from the grey haunt of herself – but then she was drawn to it again, and she returned –

The strange thing was that she looked oddly serene, and she knew that this time the separation would hold.

*

This was the summer that Dilly lit out for the territories late at night and drifted about the empty country roads alone. To be at the far end of the peninsula on a summer's night with a paleness in the sky after midnight even – it was like a sad film about an island of the north. When you know at some level that you're saying goodbye to it all. The loveliness of these bereft roads by night. The ferns in the ditches that were hardly moving but breathed in the warm night breeze, it seemed, and even spoke.

Cynthia said –

You're away with the fucking birds, Dilly. You do know that, don't you?

*

Another year passed. Another summer traipsed up from the south. They sat in the night garden and drank. In truth, it was just a rocky little field above the bay – the garden never took for her mother. There was a lone tree by the ditch, a dwarf tree twisted by the sea wind, its stunted limbs like witch's fingers. Torches were lit against the summer-night bugs, the midges that went for the neck blood especially. Charlie Redmond was parked down the road in his old Mercedes, watching the house and smoking. Every year it just got fucking crazier. She sat with her mother and they drank a bottle of blush wine and then opened another.

We should go in, Dill.

If we go in, we can't see what he's doing.

It'll be fine. We need to eat something.

He's not well, Ma. I mean the face on him?

He's okay. There's always pasta and pesto?

Like the stations of the fucking cross.

I know but it'd be quick. I was going to cook a chicken. Or like a fish. Make an effort. I was going to bake a whole fish. Some salad. Pasta and pesto is going to depress the fucking Jesus out of us.

He's down there still.

He's harmless, Dilly. He just thinks he's looking after us.

*

October. The month of slant beauty. Knives of melancholy flung in silvers from the sea. The mountains dreamed of the winter soon to come. The morning sounded hoarsely from the caverns of the bay. The birds were insane again. If she kept walking, toe to heel, one foot after the other, one end of the room to the other, the nausea kept to one side. It leered at her with a hissing threat from the one side only. The pain was yellowish and intense and abundantly fucking ominous. Cynthia knew by now that she was very sick.

*

Dilly lay back in the bed. She allowed her hand to trail down and she dreamed about some things for a while. Haunch of shoulder. Slope of thigh. Some nameless love. Some eyeless love. The winter days travelled greyly over the fields of the sea. She flexed her toes and held the stretch and tried to wish the chill from her bones. Someday I will live in the desert, she thought. I could live in a bender there, and maybe just keep a dog or two, and maybe there is someone to make a rendezvous with after dark, some long, horse-faced creature from a myth, with serpent's tail and rancid smile, a lover ardent as the night. As the cool desert breeze as it moves across our love.

She swung her legs out from beneath the covers. She was nineteen years old and obsessed with Jack Nicholson in Five Easy Pieces (the damage), with the mystical lost recordings from Lee Perry's Black Ark Studio, and with a webcam that showed the eerie view from a motorway bridge over an abandoned suburb of Tokyo. She liked the feeling beneath her bare feet of brushed concrete as she descended the stair. It was a horny feeling, like money coming in.

In the kitchen Maurice sat gauntly with his weed vaporiser and the knit bones of his smile; he was wretched and green, a sick lizard prince. Charlie lay in a foetal huddle on the sofa.

Hey now, she said.

She trailed her fingertips along the back of Maurice's neck to console. A tension shot through him in a thin, whippety snap, a cabled tension. She knew that he was suffering. Just by looking at him she could tune into the white burn of Maurice in his suffering.

Your mother's doing great, girl, he said. I was onto the hospital there again.

She's doing fabulous, Charlie said.

I mean the treatments they got now? When you think about it?

Maurice shook his head in awe.

Unbelievable, he said.

The machines they got in the hospitals now? Charlie said. It's like the Starship Enterprise out at the Cork Regional.

She's taking this thing on, Maurice said, and she's totally going to fucken beat it. You know that, Dilly, don't you?

*

The months proceeded. There was no remorse. It was summer again, and Dilly knew that it was the last one she would spend on the peninsula. On the June nights she went out to walk so as not to panic. She walked the clifftops in true dark. She sensed older presences as she walked. She knew by a cold stirring that here they had made their fires, and here their cattle had grazed, and here they ate periwinkles and oysters from the shell, and they had this burning salt on their lips, and felt this old rain, and made their cries of love and war, and roamed in hordes; their little kingdoms here were settled, and disassembled; by night, in our valley, the wolves had bayed.

*

She went into the cold seawater. A swarming light moved over the bay. A fishing boat idled far off. She basked on the rocks a while in the last heat of the day. She found her face in the shallows of a rock pool. It was woeful, proletarian, grandiose.

Down the strand there was the pattern of a family at play in the inky haze – young parents, two small kids, their chattering.

The edge of the horizon across the bay darkened.

It would be an evening of warm summer rain.

The Bull, the Cow and the Calf were ghost traces in the sea haze.

And the pattern sound of the family at play down the strand – shrieks, soft coaxing, recrimination.

In the morning her mother would be brought home from the hospital – all treatments had failed.

*

I'm not going to wait it out, Dilly.

Ah, Mam.

You know what I mean by that?

Please, she said.

Dilly, I have to go. Do you know what I mean, sweetheart?

Ah, Jesus.

Dilly, what you have to know? Is that you can't be around them. You need to go away and not come back. There's some money still.

I don't want your fucking money.

*

Drownings give onto drownings – this is everywhere in the annals, everywhere in the lore. Drownings come in patterns; they throng and cluster. The island race had a native talent for the genre.

Cynthia sat in the late afternoon and looked down on the bay and drank a glass of elderflower cordial just mildly excited by a splash of Hendrick's gin. The little taste of gin at the edges was giving her that sense of what-the-fuck. As well now as any other time.

The pain would not relent.

*

Dilly sat on the couch in the long room above the bay. There was a guard in uniform, with his cap in his hands to show a monkish bald spot, also a plain-clothes detective, and a doctor. They milled about in a kind of embarrassment and made little eye contact and, what was the phrase, the kid gloves.

Have you spoken to your father today?

That I have not.

Do you have his number?

He has different numbers.

The blue lights of emergency had spun along the coast road, across the cliffs.

202

The rescue boat was out from Berehaven, but there was no word and there would be weather overnight.

Her body would not be found.

*

She left the place in her mother's battered Saab. She drove out the sea road. A heron was the sentry to the water's shallows. It watched for movement across the fields of dull sealight. It stood perfectly still and priestly and turned its head by a clockwork nidge, mechanically. Her heart was chaotic. Her heart it was breaking.

The peninsula ran its flank along the line of the coast road. The mountain absorbed the evening light and glowed morbidly. A roadside grotto showed the blue virgin. For the souls of the vehicular dead. By ten the moon was visible and drew her strangely. A vivid, late-summer moon. A xanthic was the word moon. She stopped the car and buzzed the window to hear the breath of sea; a strimmer vexed late in a high field; somewhere too the vixen screamed. On the ribs of the sea the last of the evening sun made bone-white marks. The hills for their part vibrated royally. It was close to night and oh-so-quiet again. The stars appeared all at once – a canopy of stars clasped by tidy neutron bridges, each star an atom's core.

In new starlight she drove across the lower flanks of the Miskish. How fine it would be – don't we all sometimes think – to steal away into the sky and night. To be lifted up by those soft hands.

As she drove Dilly looked back just the once and let her lips move once to say goodbye.

*

Cynthia walked to the beach on her last night. She walked alone down a country road in that place out by the sea. The night was still and clear. As she walked she became aware of a solitary figure on the road ahead of her. Even at a distance she could tell it was a man. There was a bunched ferocity to the stance, though he was himself absolutely still, as though cut from stone, and he stared out across the fields and the hills in the direction of Berehaven.

Her step beat out against the hollows of the road, but the noise of her approach did not stir the man at all and he made the night sinister just by standing there, so still and alone.

As she came closer, she saw that the man's hands were gripped tightly to make fists. There was the sensation palpably of a violence stored. She thought that maybe it was just an old man gone in the head a bit but now he clarified.

He looked to be in his forties, neither old nor young, more stocky than slight, and his eyes were vicious and wide as he stared out across the fields and the hills in the direction of Berehaven.

She did not dare turn her eyes to the man as she passed by. She gave him a wide berth and kept her face down, but swung it low and discreetly to see that he was barefoot and his trousers were cut off at the ankles. Also, he appeared to be wet, as if he had just walked out of the sea.

Some lost pirate, it seemed, and she was certain now that the man would break his hold to spring an attack.

But all remained still, and quiet, but for her step, and but for the slow, swung chains of the sea.

She walked on down the road and along by the bay, and when she chanced a look back over her shoulder the man remained absolutely tensed and rigid, and she kept walking as she made for the beach but when she looked back again, the road was entirely empty – a void – and she walked out into the last pale dark of the night

along a jag of the bay,

by the grey musical sea,

in the place beyond Berehaven.

Chapter Fourteen

A RAINY NIGHT IN ALGECIRAS

At the port of Algeciras, in October 2018

It is night in the terminal building at the port of Algeciras. The last ferry has moved out for Tangier. There is almost nobody left on the floor. The tannoys are silent. The café bar is locked down and shuttered. Beneath the sign marked INFORMACIÓN, the desk is empty, the hatch in darkness. Along from the hatch, on the same bench, Maurice Hearne and Charlie Redmond sit together alone but for their remorse. They have the tune of it easily, by nature almost it seems.

Another thing you'd say for it, Charlie?

Is what, Maurice?

That in a sense it's a very rich taste of life you get. There's a special intensity to it.

Come again, Moss?

I mean it's as profound an experience as the world has to offer, in a way, is a broken heart.

I come from a long line of the same, Maurice. The broken-heartedness.

Is that right, Charles?

The Redmond men all wind up with the hearts busted in their boxes. It's part of the deal with us, apparently.

They look left, they look right, and in perfect tandem.

You think she can look after herself? Dilly?

It's hard to think about it. A young girl loose in these places. With the quarehawks that'd be roaming about?

She has a head on her. Is the only thing.

She has, yeah. Like the mother. There's a sly and canny element.

A tired old Maroc breastfeeds a sweeping brush. The girl locks up at the concession stand and waves to the Maroc. A security guard waddles along with all the laments of Andalusia on his brow.

Do you think about Cynthia, Maurice?

I try not to. She goes through me sometimes.

Into the middle distance they train their hard stares. There is a stock of hard knowledge to be drawn on. They know what they had once and what was lost.

I used to meet her down in the Sextant Bar, Charlie says.

This is Cynthia?

This is Cyn.

Why would you pick the Sextant?

Because it was off the path a bit. People would have to go out of their ways. You know that mostly all we'd do is sit and talk to each other.

It's the mostly is the knife in my heart, Charlie.

The sound of the night as it is heard now from the terminal at the port of Algeciras –

the murmur of the night traffic as it travels the coast road, like the drone of a hopeless prayer at the far edges of a life,

a cry that's somehow child-like from an exotic bird among the ratty palm trees outside the superSol arcade,

the low growl and the crackling of a thunderstorm as it travels ever nearer.

The men slip for their comfort onto a reminiscent line: Barrack Street, in 1986 –

Do you remember the days of the Emerald River Chinese, Charlie?

Stop it, would you? Please? We'll never get them days back, Moss.

How many Wong sisters was there for a finish?

How many Wongs does it take to make a wight?

The old jokes are best. Was there five of them?

You couldn't keep a count, Maurice. The way they was up and down Barrack Street, the Wong girls, and one of 'em gorgeouser than the next.

There was Tina?

And there was Debs.

Debs the eldest? Three others, maybe four. They would have accounted for a share of our dreams in those days, Charlie?

Of our hot and fetid dreams.

You know the worst of it, this looking back?

What's that?

The chancy ones. The ones that would have gone for it only you never tried. The ones you were afraid to have a go at.

We all have our regrets, Maurice. As older gentlemen.

You might know love again, Charlie.

I might, yeah. A little ear, nose and throat nurse from Clonmel. She'll be fucken thrilled to see me coming, I'd say.

It goes by so quickly, the moments roam, the nights give onto nights, the thunderstorm is directly above now, and a hard rain begins to fall on the port of Algeciras.

The men look up together to the high windows.

It's a heavy rain and it comes in great thundery squalls, and they have nowhere left to go but out to the streets of the port town and into it.

They walk together through the terminal. Charlie carries the Adidas hold-all and drags his soulful limp after him. They walk into the warm night air and the assault of hot rain. Maurice squints his one good eye into the rain and gauges its intensity. The men walk in the lee of the building to keep the worst of the rain off themselves.

One of our great talents, Maurice. As a people.

Which is the what, Charlie?

Is the walking close-in to buildings to keep the rain off ourselves.

We're world-beaters for it, Mr Redmond.

All these old ports have their native sadnesses. When we move by water, our hearts rise up. The roads and the narrow climbing streets are slick with rain. The colours of the street lights blur and move. The men take shelter on the port front beneath the awning of a ticket agency. Rags of faded posters – the missing. Boats for Ceuta and boats for Tangier. They stare into the rain off the Straits.

I could never have been what you were to her, Maurice.

Charlie?

I could never present myself as a serious proposition, you know?

We don't need to do this.

Ah, we kind of do, really.

I don't want to do this, Charlie.

They look in contrary directions along the port. The arclights smear above the stacks of containers. The old, dark, boxy town looms sombrely behind them – already it is dead for the night. Maurice Hearne counts the times, the years he has passed through this place. Memory trips, and Karima flits in from nowhere. Her eyes that were lit and alive and waited for him in the night until he woke, when he turned and arranged her on the bed, when he whispered conspiracies to her loins.

You wouldn't be right in yourself, Maurice.

No, Charlie.

I mean that's a night that would fucken test you now.

Charlie Redmond throws a mean squint at the sky. It has plenty to say for itself. The rain squalls and whines, and Charlie's expression is grim as he attempts to read it. He adored Cynthia the first time he saw her. When she turned the twist of a smile on him, he felt like he'd stepped off the earth.

Fuck me. It's thirty years ago nearly.

Which, Charlie?

Nothin'.

The past is uncertain, mobile. It shifts and rearranges back there. All might turn and change back there yet. It was a Sunday evening on Barrack Street that Maurice first spoke to her. There was a great stillness on the air. The cathedral bells did not pierce but made a frame for it. He crossed the street to get ahead of her. He turned and smiled, but she did not.

I'm no good at this, he said. Isn't it Cynthia?

She admitted that it was. To say anything at all was the mistake.

You're busy-looking for a Sunday, Maurice said.

He kept step with her down the hill into town. He asked if she would like to go for a drink with him at the Oval Bar. She said that she needed to get home.

But we look like a couple, he said.

He went as far as the bus station with her and leaned back against the wall and did not try to be funny.

Let me know if this is in any way getting to be an annoyance, he said.

He knew that progress was certain. Tough white gulls ran the air above the river like a precinct. She said nothing but he could see she was wondering what it would be like if they kissed.

I think it could be quite nice, he said.

And for the first time she smiled.

How the fuck did you do that? she said.

And he just kissed her.

In Algeciras the rain falls as if to wash our meagre sins away. The gutters run, the rooftops drip.

Is there any end in sight, Maurice?

This is the great unfortunate thing, Charlie. We might have a length of road to go yet.

Dragging ourselves along the fucken thing.

Like lepers. They'll be listenin' out for the little bells.

It is night again in Algeciras. The rain comes through the lights of the harbour but now more meekly. Charlie Redmond leans back beneath the jut of the ticket agent's awning. He huddles into the knit of his thin shoulders. The prospect of another November is a mean taste at the back of his throat.

Maurice Hearne steps out from the held tension of himself, he loosens up, he sticks his head out beneath the jut and gazes blankly to the night sky, there above the port and stacks, and yes, it is clearing, and the stars are the same old stars, and he turns a look to his pal that's halfways hopeful —

I think it's stopping, he says.